PRAISE FOR THE BOOKS OF
#1 INTERNATIONAL BESTSELLING AUTHOR
KERK MURRAY

Since the Day We Promised

"Books don't often make me sob, but this one did. There was an innocence and nostalgia about the story that gave me all the feels."
— Reader Review

"I have only two words for this series and this book in particular. Absolutely amazing!"
— Reader Review

"What a finale. I am glad to have read and enjoyed all six books."
— Reader Review

Since the Day We Left

"Haven't cried that hard over a book in a long time."

— Reader Review

"I read this in one sitting on a rainy weekend and it was PERFECT. Already ordered copies for my book club."

— Reader Review

"I picked up this book on a whim and now I'm ordering everything Kerk Murray has ever written."

— Reader Review

Since the Day We Wished

"I read it in one sitting! If you love small town romance with realistic characters, you need to read this. I already pre-ordered the next one."

— Reader Review

"Loved every page. The Wishing Tree concept was so romantic and unique. Kerk Murray is an auto-buy author for me now."
— Reader Review

"I hope this gets made into a movie. So good!"
— Reader Review

Since the Day We Kissed

"This is the first romance I've read written by a male and won't be my last by this author. His take on romance was surprisingly insightful—you can't help but cheer for Kara and Ethan."
— Reader Review

"The best story in the series by far!"
— Reader Review

"I can't wait to read more Kerk Murray books! He's my favorite new-to-me author."
— Reader Review

Since the Day We Fell

"Hadley Cove feels like a character in itself. It's a place that feels both real and magical and one that I never want to leave."

— Reader Review

"Kerk has a gift for capturing the nuances of human emotion. I found myself stopping to highlight several passages."

— Reader Review

"I've been a fan of Kerk's work since *Pawprints On Our Hearts*, and *Since the Day We Fell* did not disappoint."

— Reader Review

Since the Day We Danced

"Murray's writing is simply gorgeous."
— The Book Commentary

"An emotional rollercoaster that will make you fall in love with love all over again."

— Reader Review

"A beautiful escapist Nicholas Sparks type romance."

— Reader Review

Pawprints On Our Hearts

"Animal lovers will feel connected to Murray's almost spiritual awakening and admire his devotion to following his heart, even in the face of tremendous sacrifice. This touching memoir overflows with intense emotion."

— Booklife by Publishers Weekly

"A deeply moving memoir... one of the best books that capture the connection between human beings and dogs... *Pawprints on Our Hearts* inspires a love for animals while exploring the painful edges of the human heart in need of love and healing."

BY KERK MURRAY

Dog Lovers Series

Pawprints On Our Hearts
Little Black Dog

Hadley Cove Sweet Romance Series

Since the Day We Danced
Since the Day We Fell
Since the Day We Kissed
Since the Day We Wished
Since the Day We Left
Since the Day We Promised

Sugarberry Ridge Holiday Romance Series

The Christmas Angel
The Christmas Star
The Christmas Wish
The Christmas Miracle
The Christmas Train
The Christmas Cottage

Since the Day We Promised

KERK MURRAY

Since the Day We Promised

Hadley Cove Sweet Romance: Book 6

Magnolia Press
Birmingham

Magnolia Press
105 Vulcan Rd
Ste 221
Birmingham, AL 35209

Library of Congress Cataloging-in-Publication Data

Names: Murray, Kerk, author.
Title: Since the Day We Promised/ Kerk Murray.
Description: First edition. | Birmingham: Magnolia Press, 2025.
Identifiers: LCCN 2025920505 | ISBN 9798992553833 (paperback) | ISBN 9798992553840 (hardcover)

Printed in the United States of America

For those who need a second chance
—this one's for you.

Before You Begin...

You're invited to join my private Facebook Reader Group, where you'll make new book friends, meet other animal lovers, and be the first to know about new releases, book clubs, and special deals.

Join today:
Kerk Murray's private Facebook Reader Group

facebook.com/groups/779562103953550

Story Playlist

Listen on your favorite music streaming platform.

kerkmurray.com/products/sincethedaywepromisedplaylis
t

Liam's Listens

♪♫♪

1. "I'll Be Seeing You" — Billie Holiday

2. "Blue Moon" — Frank Sinatra

3. "Unchained Melody" — Les Baxter

4. "Stand By Me" — Ben E. King

5. "Earth Angel" — The Penguins

6. "In the Still of the Night" — The Five Satins

7. "Tennessee Waltz" — Patti Page

8. "Cry" — Johnnie Ray

9. "Only You" — The Platters

10. "Love Me Tender" — Elvis Presley

Amelia's Listens

♪♫

1. "Dream a Little Dream of Me" — Ella Fitzgerald

2. "La Vie En Rose" — Édith Piaf

3. "Secret Love" — Doris Day

4. "Moonlight Serenade" — Glenn Miller

5. "Que Sera, Sera" — Doris Day

6. "At Last" — Etta James

7. "I Only Have Eyes for You" — The Flamingos

8. "Young at Heart" — Frank Sinatra

9. "Autumn Leaves" — Nat King Cole

10. "Love Is a Many-Splendored Thing" — The Four Aces

Dear Reader,

Welcome to where it all began—Hadley Cove, 1948.

As I wrote this story, I found myself reflecting on the promises we make and the extraordinary power they hold over our entire lives.

You'll meet young Liam and Amelia, whose friendship blooms under a pecan tree and whose story spans years of separation and hope.

And my hope is that as you follow Liam's journey from a scared eight-year-old to the wise storyteller we meet at Second Chance Rescue, you'll perhaps recognize a piece of your own childhood. I invite you to consider the promises you've made, the people who shaped you, and the enduring truth that some love is worth waiting a lifetime for.

Thank you for being a part of this incredible adventure and for joining me in creating a more compassionate world for all living beings, one heartwarming story at a time.

Your support through reading and sharing this series, along with your kind words in messages and reviews, means more than I can express. I'm forever grateful.

Don't forget to check out the extras I've included at the front and end of the book, created with you in mind.

PS. Keep in mind that though this is the sixth and final book in this series, it's the prequel and takes place before *Since the Day We Danced.*

"We are all in the gutter,
but some of us are looking at the stars."

—Oscar Wilde, *Lady Windermere's Fan*

1

Saturday

THERE IT WAS ... Fourteen twenty-two Muscadine Drive.

Liam Wright shut off the engine and sat there for a minute, resting his hands on the wheel of his old Ford F1. Through the windshield, webbed with old cracks he'd always meant to fix, he studied the house he'd built with his own two hands.

His granddaughter, Emma, and her husband, Chad, lived here now. He'd given it to Emma as a wedding gift, not long after her grandmother had died. It felt right passing along the place that had seen decades of birthdays, scraped knees, and muddy shoes by the door. He'd since moved to a smaller place on the water. Easier to manage. Easier on the heart.

Emma had done a fine job taking care of the place. The dark-brown wood had aged with grace. Those forest-green shutters he'd painted and repainted more times than he could count still hung straight. The wraparound porch, where he'd taught Emma to tie her shoes and sat through summer storms, made the place feel exactly as a home should. Loved. Looked after.

Of course, that was all Emma's doing.

In all the years she'd been with Chad, Liam couldn't recall seeing that boy mow the grass even once. Emma kept the lawn trimmed, the hedges neat, and the flower beds blooming along the walkway. It all fell on her shoulders, and it pained him. She deserved more. But if he'd learned anything over the years, it was that he couldn't change anyone or change things for them. He could only love them and hope that was enough.

As he climbed out of the truck, his knees reminded him he wasn't twenty. Wasn't even seventy anymore, for that matter. His eyes roamed over its Meadow Green paint that had faded over the years—more gray-green now than anything—but she still ran like the day he'd gotten her.

When he took a breath, the June morning air hit him like a warm, damp blanket. Humidity clung to him, plastering his shirt to his back.

This hot already?

It wasn't even nine o'clock yet.

In coastal Georgia, summers arrived in April and didn't let up until October. Seemed like the summers had gotten worse every year, or maybe it just felt that way after eighty-two years on this earth.

Eighty-two?

Somewhere after thirty-five, he'd stopped counting.

As Liam walked up the stone path, he glanced at the empty spot in the driveway where Chad usually parked his red Camaro. Only Emma's little Honda sat beneath the carport.

The front door was wide open.

"Em? Are you in here?" Liam called out, poking his head through the screen door.

"Upstairs, Grandpa! I'll be down in two!"

He stepped inside and closed the door behind him. "Okay. I'll be here."

Liam walked into the living room and over to the fireplace. As he looked at the photographs on the mantelpiece, he smiled at one of Emma with her friend, Lisa, at what looked like a wine tasting, both of them holding half-empty glasses and laughing. He'd always liked Lisa—she'd been a good friend to Emma for as long as he could remember.

Next to it sat a favorite photo of him and Emma when she was maybe seven or eight, both of them grinning at the camera with the ocean behind them. One of her small hands was curled into his; the other clutched a bright green bucket. A half-built, lopsided sandcastle leaned in the foreground—clearly the work of two proud amateurs.

As his eyes continued along the mantel, he paused.

Emma and Chad's wedding photo was missing.

Maybe she moved it. Or maybe ...

He didn't know the reason—but still, he noticed.

"I'm almost ready!" Emma called from upstairs. "Just have to grab a few boxes from the kitchen, then we can go!"

"Okay, dear! Is there anything I can do to help?"

"No, no. Be there in a sec ... have to find my other shoe."

Liam turned back to the fireplace and ran his hand along the piece of wood he'd fixed to the brick wall years ago. His fingers traced the rough outline of a heart carved into the grain.

Inside it, the initials remained: *A + L.*

He smiled, remembering the afternoon he'd carved them decades ago ...

Blue sundress.

Auburn curls.

Sunlight beneath the pecan tree—

"Okay, ready!" Emma clattered down the stairs, and Liam blinked as she grabbed boxes on her way through the kitchen. "Just got a few deliveries in Savannah after I drop you off."

Liam reached for a box. "Let me help you with those."

"I've got it, Grandpa," she said, but he was already prying one free from her hands.

"I might be older than the marsh grass at low tide, but I still walk three miles every morning. These bones have some strength left in them, you know."

"I know, I know." Emma chuckled. "You've done enough for me already."

"I'd do anything for my Em."

Their eyes met for a moment before he walked over to the front door and held it open for her. "So the dog treat business is doing well?"

She blew out a breath and breezed past him. "I don't know if I'd say well ... but I'm selling some boxes here and there."

"Some are better than none. Don't sell yourself short. I think you've got a good thing going. And I've never heard any complaints from the dogs at the rescue," Liam said as they walked to her car.

Emma popped the trunk, and they loaded the boxes inside, arranging them so they wouldn't slide around during the drive. He smiled at how carefully she'd labeled each one in her neat handwriting.

That handwriting? Sure didn't come from my side.

"Grandpa." Emma glanced over at his truck. "When's the last time you got the oil changed in that thing?"

"March fifteenth. Three thousand two hundred miles ago. Had the points and plugs checked, greased all the fittings, and the brakes adjusted. I rotate the tires myself every six months."

"You shouldn't be rotating your own tires at your age—"

"If I quit doing things just because 'I shouldn't,' I'd be sitting in a rocking chair talking to squirrels."

Emma shook her head, but couldn't hide her smile. "We could go look at something new, you know. Something with air conditioning that actually works. Maybe some of those modern safety features—"

"Don't need all those bells and whistles. I don't want something new. She may not look like much, but she gets me to where I need to go."

Emma laughed and closed the trunk. "All right, all right. But if that thing breaks down on you ..."

"It won't."

After they got into the car and Emma started to drive, Liam sensed she had something on her mind. He waited a few blocks, watching the trees blur past the window, before speaking up. They rolled to a stop at a red light.

"Did you two have another fight?"

Emma glanced over at him. "No. Of course not. What makes you say that?"

"Well, the front door was wide open when I got there. And I—"

"He forgot something at work, that's all." She looked away. "Left in a hurry."

Liam thought about mentioning the missing wedding photo from the mantelpiece, but decided against it. If she'd moved it, she had her reasons. There was something she wasn't telling him, but he'd learned better than to press—Emma was like her grandmother that way. He'd have to wait for her to come to him.

———

As they pulled into Second Chance Rescue, the familiar sound of barking and the songs of mockingbirds in the towering live oak welcomed them. Liam smiled at the sight of the building that had become a second home. The cottage-style structure looked inviting, with its bright red front door and clean white shutters. Flower boxes beneath each window spilled over with purple petunias and trailing ivy—Emma had helped plant those last spring. Just above the entrance, a brass plaque etched with the silhouettes of a cat and a dog glinted in the morning sun.

The moment they stepped inside, Kara looked up from behind the counter where she was wiping down the surface. Her face lit up. "Em! Liam! Good to see y'all again." She came around the desk and pulled them both into a quick hug. "Charlotte's here in the back—"

"Liam!"

Charlotte came bounding through a set of doors to the

side of them, her ponytail swinging and sneakers skidding on the tile.

"Hello young lady." Liam opened his arms, and she wrapped him in a quick hug. "How's school?"

Charlotte groaned, rolling her eyes. "Ugh, it's school. But I'm surviving."

"You're the spitting image of your mama, you know that? Got her smile. And that same look when you talk about something you don't like."

"She gets that from years of dealing with me, poor thing." Kara flung an arm over her chest like she was in an old soap opera.

Charlotte smirked. "It's not so bad. We make a good team."

"That we do." Kara gave her a quick squeeze, then faced Liam. "Your storytelling has been such a hit with our Rescue Reader program. Honestly, you've been a godsend to us. The animals calm right down when you start reading. I swear you're like the 'animal whisperer' or something."

He waved her off with a chuckle. "Oh, come on now. I just read to them, that's all."

Kara gestured toward her daughter. "Don't be so modest. Charlotte here tells everyone about the voices you do for different characters."

"Well, I can't imagine doing anything else with all the time I have on my hands these days. Besides, I think I enjoy it as much as they do."

Emma smiled. "He does have a lovely voice for it, doesn't he?"

Liam gently nudged her arm. "Don't you have some boxes to deliver?"

"I do," she said with a sigh. "But I'll be back. Shouldn't take long if I-95 ain't too crazy. See y'all later!"

After they all waved their goodbyes to Emma, Kara turned to Liam and Charlotte. "Well, shall we see what story we're reading today?" She led them over to the bookcase and sorted through the titles—*Charlotte's Web*, *The Incredible Journey*, *Shiloh*, *Stuart Little*.

"I wish we had a new story to read." Charlotte frowned at her mom.

"You'll survive," Kara said. "We can just read one of these again. You love Charlotte's Web."

Charlotte shrugged. "Well, yeah—I mean, it does have my name in it."

"Hard to compete with a classic like that." Liam grinned, then surveyed the books again. "You know what? Maybe I won't read a story today. I can share one I know—by heart."

Charlotte tilted her head. "Like ... one you made up?"

"Now this I've got to hear." Kara folded her arms.

"You won't find it on any bestseller list." Liam rubbed the back of his neck. "But it's one I've carried around with me for quite some time now."

His mind drifted to the initials carved on the mantelpiece: *A + L*. He closed his eyes for a moment, and could almost smell her lavender perfume. Her laughter echoing as he chased her around that old pecan tree. The warmth of her small hand in his after he'd finally caught her.

Liam opened his eyes. "Let's gather the animals and bring them into the reading area."

Kara glanced at the clipboard on the shelf. "We have a

few volunteers today, plus some folks looking to adopt who might want to listen in. Is that okay?"

"The more the merrier."

After everyone had chosen an animal for the Rescue Reader program, they made their way into the reading room. The cozy space was a patchwork of overstuffed sofas and chairs arranged in a loose semicircle. Charlotte settled on the floor with Whiskers, the tabby cat, purring in her lap, while a volunteer sat nearby with Danni, a cocker spaniel, snuggled against her side. Another volunteer held Snowball, a white rabbit that twitched her nose at all the activity. A few potential adopters had joined them—one with Scout, a border collie, sitting at his feet, and another gently petting Marmalade, an orange cat that had claimed the arm of her chair.

Liam eased himself into an old recliner and looked toward the corner, where a golden retriever rested inside a crate. A volunteer sat by the dog, who was still too anxious to join everyone else. Liam caught the dog's eye and gave him a reassuring smile. "Don't worry, Riley boy. You can listen from right there."

Once everyone had settled in, the room fell into silence. All eyes shifted to Liam. Even the animals seemed to lean in.

His throat closed. His breath snagged halfway between his chest and the ache of remembering. Every yesterday. Every tomorrow. Every version of the life he might've lived. Somehow, all at once, right there with him.

Not today. I can't do this.

He glanced around at the expectant faces: Kara, Charlotte, the volunteers, the animals. They were all waiting—for a story, yes, but also for *him*.

Sunlight streamed through the windows, but it was the single stained-glass panel near the back that caught his attention. Shades of gold and violet shimmered across the floor. For a split second, he could almost see her standing there—arms crossed, a half-smile on her face, and that look that always told him: *you've got this*.

The lump in his throat didn't vanish, but something steadied inside him.

"Well," he said, voice slightly hoarse. "Here goes nothing."

Another pause.

He looked down at his hands and held still.

Then, as the moment found him, he drew a measured breath and lifted his gaze to the faces gathered before him.

"It was 1948 ..."

2

Spring 1948

Tommy Ashford slammed Liam into the schoolyard fence just as the final bell rang. The chain-link rattled against his back, knocking the breath clean out of him. Most of the other eight-year-olds had already run for the buses, but Liam wasn't that lucky.

"Look at them raggedy clothes." Tommy jabbed a finger at Liam's patched-up shirt. "That shirt's got more holes than my daddy's old shrimp net."

Liam winced and cradled his ribs as he stepped sideways, trying to slip past the bigger boy. "Just leave me be."

"What's that, poor boy?" Tommy yanked Liam's collar, splitting the shirt at the shoulder. "Heard your daddy ran from them Germans, caught one in the back—like a coward."

Something fierce erupted in Liam's chest.

Nobody's gonna talk about my Pa like that.

His fists clenched. He swung with everything he had. Air whooshed past.

Missed.

Tommy didn't. His fist cracked against Liam's face.

Liam hit the dirt hard and his shirt snagged on a rock, ripping wider as he rolled. The taste of copper filled his mouth.

One of Tommy's friends spat on Liam. "That's what cowards' sons get."

The older boys walked away, still snickering. Liam pushed himself up, head spinning. He didn't look back at the fence; he just started walking.

On the dusty road home, he touched his mouth. His fingers came away bloody. He stared down, then ran his hand across his shirt—felt the torn fabric, the loose threads, the flap where the shoulder used to be. It was hanging off him like laundry on the line.

Ma's gonna be mad. This was my good shirt.

The mile walk to fourteen twenty-two Muscadine Drive felt more like ten. Liam's lip throbbed, and every step sent a spike of pain through his scraped knee. The other kids were right about one thing—his clothes were raggedy. Hand-me-downs from the church donation box, patched and re-patched until they were more thread than fabric.

Tommy and his friends always had new things. Clean shirts. Pants that reached their shoes. Polished shoes that weren't falling apart. Tommy's daddy drove a big shiny car and wore a suit to work. Liam had seen him at the general store once, buying whatever he wanted without counting coins like Ma did. Tommy probably never had to wear dead folks' clothes or worry that his shoes wouldn't see him through the winter.

Sometimes Liam wondered why some folks got all the nice things and others just had to make do. Was it luck? Or was the world just built that way?

As he passed the neighboring property, he spotted a couple of fancy cars and some trucks in the drive of the big farmhouse. It wasn't just big—it looked important, the kind of house folks slowed down to stare at. That place had been empty for years. Ma had always said it was a shame the farm went untended, since it had some of the best land in the area.

When he finally reached home, Liam nudged open the screen door—and stopped.

No cooking? No radio?

Ma sat at the kitchen table with her friend, Mrs. Patterson, both of them hunched over steaming cups of coffee.

"—fired me this morning," Ma said, dabbing at her cheek with a tissue. "Said it was budget cuts, but we both know it's what folks been whisperin' about William."

"Oh, Mary." Mrs. Patterson reached across and squeezed her hand. "Don't pay them folks no mind. Ain't nothing meaner than a bored mouth."

"I begged him not to go and fight their war." Ma shook her head. "But he said if he didn't, they'd run him right outta town."

Mrs. Patterson nodded. "It was hard on all our Hadley Cove boys. They went, scared or not, 'cause they felt like they had to."

Ma looked down at her coffee. Her voice was quiet when she spoke again. "And yeah, it's true. He ran. He got shot in the back. But I know my William. He was just tryin' to get back home to me and Liam." Her chin trembled. "War always ends the same way: the rich start it, and folks like us pay the price."

Mrs. Patterson's gaze didn't leave Ma's. "Our General Lee had it right—said it's a good thing war's so awful, or we'd go fallin' in love with it. But it's the women left behind to carry what's left. And the truth don't make it hurt any less. So what now, Mary? What're you gonna do?"

Ma drew in a shaky breath. "I don't know, Helen. That Army money helps a bit." She gave a dry, joyless laugh. "They send me that little check every month, like fifty-two bucks and a typed-up apology is all his life came down to. And they think that's enough. They think it's okay to do this to us."

Ma's voice broke. "How am I supposed to take care of Liam? His toes are stickin' right out the front of them shoes. And he's eatin' like a plow horse lately. And what if he gets sick? Dr. Rutledge charges a dollar just to walk through the door, and that's if you can get him to come out here."

Liam hadn't planned to stand there for so long. He should've turned around. Should've walked back out like he hadn't heard a thing. But his books slid from his hands and hit the floor with a thud that made both women jump.

"Liam!" Ma shot to her feet, wiping at her face. Her eyes were red as apples. "I didn't hear you come in. What happened to—"

He couldn't take it.

Not the look on Ma's face. Not the way her voice cracked.

He bolted. The screen door clapped behind him as he flew over the fence and raced through the field. Behind him, his Ma's voice called out, growing fainter with each step. "Liam! Come back! Liam!"

Her voice followed him, but he didn't stop. His torn shirt flapped in the wind. His lungs screamed. The pecan tree grew larger—closer with every stride.

Almost there.

His legs gave out just as he reached it. He dropped to his knees, then collapsed against the trunk. His chest heaved. His face burned. He gulped for air like he might never catch it again. The bark scraped his spine, but the shade seemed to dull the sting of the day. He leaned his head back and let his eyes drift shut. The smell of earth and green things filled his nose. Somewhere above, a mockingbird called out and then quieted.

For a moment, there was only the sound of his breath and the rustle of leaves.

Then—something. Close. Real close.

A soft hiccup. A sniffle.

He tilted his head, straining to listen.

The breeze shifted, and there it was again. A muffled sob.

He eased himself upright, holding his breath, and crept toward the sound.

The crying grew clearer.

He rounded the tree—

And the world stopped.

3

SHE WAS THE PRETTIEST girl Liam had ever seen.

The girl sat against the far side of the pecan tree, legs bent and arms looped around her knees. Sunlight caught in her long auburn curls, her pale-yellow dress, and the blue sash tied at her waist. Even with tears on her cheeks and dirt on her dress, she looked like she'd wandered straight from a fairytale.

For a long moment, Liam just stood there, taking it all in. *What's she doing here?*

He stepped closer, a twig breaking under his foot.

Her head snapped up.

"Hey. Why are you crying?" he asked.

"My daddy yelled at me." The girl hiccupped. "I didn't want to play piano today. I already played yesterday, for a whole hour, but he said that wasn't enough."

Liam crouched beside her and placed a hand on her shoulder. "Please don't cry. Maybe he just wants to hear you play because it makes him proud."

The girl hiccupped again. "You think so? I always figured he just wanted me to play good for the people who come over."

"Yeah, probably. Ma taught me to play Pa's old tabor pipe. Said it was mine now. Sometimes we play on the porch 'til the mosquitoes chase us back inside."

"What happened to you? Your clothes are—"

"Fight at school. Older boys said stuff about Pa. And Ma's been cryin' too." Liam turned his face away, staring off across the field back toward his house. "Ma always said Pa planted this tree with his own daddy when he was little and that a part of him would always be here, waiting if I ever needed him."

"I'm sorry about that."

Then, a pair of thin arms wrapped around his shoulders. She was hugging him. It was the kind of hug that made him forget, for a second, everything else that hurt. He hugged her back, breathing in her curls—a soft, sweet scent that reminded him of flowers he couldn't name.

"Why's your mom sad?"

"Lost her job at Mr. Hal's store."

"Well, we have to cheer her up. That's what you do for the people you love when they're sad."

Liam sighed. "But how?"

She tapped her finger against her lip.

Just then, a pecan dropped right onto Liam's head.

"Ow!" It bounced into his lap as he reached up to rub the spot.

She burst into giggles, then covered her mouth with her hand. "Oh! Are you hurt?"

"I'm fine." Liam grinned, picking up the pecan, then glared at the branch above. "But that gave me an idea—we could bring her pecans!"

"Does she like them?"

"She loves them. Reminds her of Pa."

The girl stood and looked up. "Then let's get her some."

"Good idea. You stay. I'll climb."

Liam brushed off his palms and made his way up the trunk. His knee stung and his back still ached, but he pushed on. He'd climbed this tree a hundred times, but it felt different with her watching—a little harder, maybe, but also more fun.

About halfway up, he glanced down. She'd gathered up her dress hem like a bowl, ready to catch whatever he dropped.

He smiled and reached for a cluster of pecans. One by one, he picked them and tossed them down. Within minutes, her makeshift basket was full.

"Okay, that's enough!" She laughed. "I don't think I can fit anymore."

Without a word, Liam started back down. When his feet finally hit the ground, he brushed his hands on his pants and stepped beside her. He grabbed a few pecans from her pile and stuffed them into his pockets. "Here. That should help." He glanced at the rest, still gathered in the folds of her dress. "You sure you got them?"

The girl nodded. "Uh-huh. Where's your house?"

"Right over the fence. This way."

They made their way across the open stretch between the tree and the fence. She moved fast, even with her dress full of pecans, weaving around briars and patches of wild grass. Liam kept his eyes on her the entire way, though he couldn't have said why.

She slipped through the fence rails, and he jumped over them. A few pecans tumbled from his pockets and disappeared into the weeds. He let them go.

That was fine, he figured. Ma would still have plenty.

———ells———

Liam stepped up to the back porch and opened the door to the kitchen. "Ma?"

She hurried in from the hallway. Her eyes were still red, but dry now. When she saw him, her face changed. "Lord have mercy, Liam! What happened to your face? And look at that shirt!"

Liam looked down at himself, as if noticing the dirt, the ripped shirt, and the dried blood for the first time. He opened his mouth to explain, but nothing came out.

Ma rushed over, grabbing a rag from the counter and dampening it at the pump. She glanced at the girl, but then turned her attention to her son. "Come here, sugar. Let me fix you up." She tilted his chin up and started dabbing at his bloody lip. "Was it them boys at school again?"

Liam flinched as the rag touched his cut. "Yes, ma'am."

Ma's jaw tightened. "Looks like I'm gonna have to talk to Mrs. Finley again. Somethin's gotta change."

"No, Ma, it'll be fine—"

"Fine?" Ma stepped back and looked him up and down. "That's not what it's lookin' like. Your face ain't fine and that shirt sure ain't fine." She shook her head. "This can't keep happenin'."

Liam shifted his weight from one foot to the other. "Ma,

please. It's okay."

"That shirt's about had it." Ma sighed and set down the rag. "I'll see if I can fix it up later." Her voice softened. "Now, what've you got stuffed in them pockets?"

Liam walked over to the kitchen table and emptied his pockets onto the wooden surface. The girl followed and emptied her dress beside his pile.

"We got these for you 'cause you were sad." Liam looked down at the pecans scattered across the table. "It was her idea, really."

Ma smiled, maybe for the first time all day. "Well, would you look at that! These look mighty fine. That was real thoughtful of you two." She gave the girl a once-over, then shot Liam a knowing look. "I'm sure your friend has a name, Liam."

His face grew hot. He'd been so caught up in everything, he'd never even asked.

"Amelia, ma'am." She made a curtsy, holding up the sides of her dress.

Liam smiled. "That's a real pretty name."

Amelia looked down, blushing and fiddling with the hem of her dress. "I like yours too."

"Well, ain't that sweet. I'm Mary, honey. Liam's ma." She smiled and brushed a stray crumb from the counter and nodded toward the door. "Now, how 'bout you two go play while I whip up somethin' sweet for y'all?"

───ℓℓ───

The sun had sunk lower in the sky. Its golden light glowed

in a way that made even their modest yard look pretty. Liam glanced around, then turned to her with a grin. "Wanna play Statues?"

"Oh! I know that one!" Amelia clapped her hands. "May I be 'it' first?"

"Sure!"

She turned around and called, "Go!" Liam dashed toward her, his bare feet slapping the dirt. "Stop!" He froze, wobbling on one foot with his arms spread out wide.

Amelia giggled. "You look just like a scarecrow!"

They played for a while—running, laughing, switching turns—until they were both out of breath. Between rounds, Liam told her about his favorite places. "There's a creek past them pines where I catch frogs. And when it gets dark, lightning bugs come out of the woods."

"Really? I ain't—I mean, I haven't ever seen lightning bugs before."

"If we wait a little, they'll come out. You'll see."

The screen door creaked open behind them and Ma popped her head out. "Kids, come on in!"

Liam shrugged. "Maybe next time. They'll be here tomorrow."

The smell hit before they reached the porch—warm maple and toasted pecans. Ma had set out a plate of steaming muffins, with two sweating glasses of ice-cold lemonade.

As they sat on the back porch steps, Liam bit into the savory treat and closed his eyes. The maple syrup Ma had drizzled on top was sticky-sweet, and the pecans crunched between his teeth.

Amelia grinned mid-bite. "This is the best thing I've ever eaten!"

They reached for their lemonade at the same time. Liam took a gulp, the cold so sharp it made his teeth ache. He winced and puckered. Amelia drank even faster, and a stream ran down her chin. She laughed and wiped it away with the back of her hand.

Ma gave them both a look over the rim of her glass. "Well now, it ain't a race. That lemonade ain't goin' nowhere."

They munched away, listening to the crickets chirping, a bullfrog croaking, and off in the distance, the steady song of a whippoorwill.

"Where do you live, Amelia?" Ma asked, refilling their glasses.

Amelia looked toward the fence. "Over there, across the farm. That white house."

"Oh, that's a lovely place." Ma wiped her hands on her apron and straightened a dish towel hanging on the railing. "You kids finish up, and then Liam, I want you to walk Amelia home. It's gettin' dark, and I don't want her parents to worry."

⸺ꝏ⸺

As Liam and Amelia crossed the field, the white house rose higher with every step, until it felt like it might swallow the sky.

"Whoa," Liam said as they arrived out front, tilting his head up. "This place is huge. Like a castle or somethin'."

White columns reached all the way to the roof, and there

were more windows than Liam could count. Big, shiny cars lined the drive. The grass looked too perfect to be real, like someone had painted it on. He stopped at the edge, unsure if he should even step on it.

He decided not to.

Amelia looked down, kicking at a pebble. "It's not all that great. It's too big. You never know where anybody is."

"You go to school here?" Liam asked, still staring up at the wide porch with all its carved railings.

"Kind of. I used to go to a girls' school in New York. But now Daddy's got a private teacher for me while we're down here."

Liam blinked. "Oh. How long are y'all stayin'?"

Amelia shrugged. "I don't know. But it's nice having a real friend here." She smoothed the folds of her dress. "Do you think we could meet at the tree tomorrow?"

4

Summer 1948

"BETCHA CAN'T CATCH ME!" Amelia called out, sprinting ahead.

Liam raced after her, both laughing as they bounded through the morning air toward the fields near his house. The fields weren't wild anymore. Not like before. That spring, men had come with loud machines and sharp tools, cutting down the weeds and chopping up the brush. Long rows of tobacco now stretched in their place across the dirt.

Up ahead, Amelia's dress fluttered in the breeze.

It was strange to think that a few months ago, he hadn't even known she existed. Now he couldn't imagine a single day without her ...

———

They'd spent every day together since meeting three months back. With school out, there was nothing to stop them from starting their days at dawn and playing until the lightning bugs came out.

Most days blurred together, but certain moments stayed with him.

There was the time Amelia had brought a book of fairy-tales from her bedroom along with her, and they'd spent the afternoon under the pecan tree taking turns reading aloud to each other. Liam stumbled over some of the bigger words, but Amelia never made him feel dumb. Instead, she smiled, tapping the page, and helped him sound the word out. Afterward, they'd make up endings of their own, usually more far-fetched than the originals.

Then there was the evening he'd finally convinced her to climb all the way to the top of the oak by the creek. She'd been terrified at first, but when they reached the highest branch, she'd laughed and said, "I can see all the stars from up here!" There was something about the way she looked at the sky that made Liam believe anything was possible—even for a boy like him. They stayed up there, dreaming about all the places they might go someday, until Ma had called him back in.

And just last week, he'd brought out his tabor pipe and taught her how to play a simple tune. Her fingers moved more graceful than his, and she picked it up so quick that by evening, she was playing melodies he'd never heard before. He didn't know how she did it, but somehow, she played as if the music already lived inside her.

Along the way, Liam picked up bits and pieces about why Amelia was in Hadley Cove. Her daddy was "in business," though she didn't know exactly what that meant.

One afternoon, they were teetering across a row of fallen logs on the creek, looking for turtles, when Amelia wiped her hands on her dress and said, "Mom's been having people over almost every week since we got the house fixed up. Important folks from Savannah and Atlanta." She balanced on the log, lifting her arms and tiptoed forward. "She says it's for Daddy's work, but mostly they eat fancy food and talk about boring stuff."

Liam eased his way along the other log, wobbling while his thoughts wandered. He pictured their chipped dishes at home and how he'd help Ma rinse them each night, then lay them out to dry on a folded feed sack by the back door. They didn't have a cupboard, just a couple of shelves Ma had nailed up years before. One night, he'd asked if they'd ever get more, and Ma had smiled and said, "Ain't but two of us, sugar. We got what we need, and that's enough."

Amelia had said something else a few days later that stuck with him too.

"We got other houses," she'd told him while they picked blackberries by the old rail line. "One in the mountains, and a big one by the ocean up north. But Daddy says this one might be the most important."

Liam rolled a berry between his fingers, watching the juice stain his thumb purple.

More than one house? For just the three of them?

He let the berry fall and looked toward the end of the rail line, where it curved into the trees and disappeared.

Don't see how a house could be more important. Ain't it just where you sleep?

His mind had drifted to the storm that had ripped shingles off their roof. Rain leaked into both bedrooms, and his mattress got soaked. Ma dragged it outside, but by nightfall it stank. "No good now," she'd said, giving him her bed. That night, she'd made herself a place by the stove, stuffing an old quilt with cotton scraps and worn-out clothes. She'd been sleeping on it ever since. Sometimes, it didn't even feel like the house belonged to them. Just a place they tried to keep holding together.

———*ele*———

"Liam!" Amelia's voice yanked him back.

He looked up just in time to see her take off, darting between the droopy green leaves. They were already up to his waist. Just past them, he could see yellow squash flowers blooming and skinny okra sticking up in the dirt. He stepped between the rows, careful not to crush anything, and followed her.

Amelia dropped into a crouch, motioning for him to get low. "Shh ... someone's coming."

Liam caught up and kneeled beside her. The leaves brushed his arms as he leaned in close.

Ahead, two men were walking down the rows. One was thin, wearing a dark suit. The other wore overalls and a straw hat. He had a notepad in his hand.

"That's my daddy," Amelia whispered. "And that's Simeon. He runs the farm."

Her daddy pointed toward something in the distance. "Think you'll have that done by Friday?"

"Yes, sir, Mr. Jensen," Simeon said, jotting a note. Then he turned toward the nearby workers. "All right, boys. Finish up this row, and move on to the squash. And I'll need y'all here an hour earlier tomorrow. We've got more beds to prep before week's end."

A few men nodded. Liam counted them—six, scattered through the rows. Some looked young, maybe like the older boys at church. Others had gray hair. Their shirts were already damp with sweat, and it wasn't even noon. One man pushed himself up with a grunt. He was tall—*taller than Pa would've been*, Liam thought. The man wiped his hands on his pants and said, "Yes, sir," in a quiet voice.

When the man turned around, he looked right at where Liam and Amelia were hiding. Liam held his breath.

Did he see us?

The man's eyes stared for what felt like forever. But then he just went back to touching the tobacco leaves—real gentle—the same way Ma touched his forehead when he had a fever.

Liam watched the men work and wondered if they got tired standing out in the sun all day. Ma always said fieldwork was hard. These men moved slow but steady. Seemed like they'd been doing it all their lives.

Simeon followed Mr. Jensen deeper into the rows. "The new drainage ditches should be finished tomorrow morning." His voice had changed, more proper now.

"Good. And how does the tobacco look to you?"

"Hard to say for certain, sir. This being our first year with it." Simeon flipped a page in his notepad. "The leaves are coming in thick, but I won't know if we're doing it right until harvest."

"The county agent said we should expect decent results if

we follow his recommendations." Mr. Jensen scratched the back of his neck. "Think we'll have enough quality leaf to interest the buyers?"

"I hope so, sir. That fertilizer mix from the extension office seems to be working. Same with the curing barn changes. It all should help." Simeon paused, staring at the rows, one hand on his hip like Ma did when she was thinking hard. "Course, won't know until we try to dry our first batch."

Liam didn't move as the men disappeared into the green.

Amelia stood and brushed off her knees. "Come on. Let's go to the creek."

Liam followed her, both slipping between the plants until they hit the edge of the field and ducked into the trees. Amelia sped up, arms out like wings, her braid bouncing behind her. Sunlight filtered down in soft patches. The air turned cooler, and the smell of mud and moss wrapped around them. Bugs buzzed somewhere up high, but the creek was louder. Then—something else.

Liam stopped. "Wait. Did you hear that?"

Amelia spun. "Hear what?"

Liam tilted his head, listening. The creek bubbled over the rocks. "There."

They both froze. A faint sound floated through the trees. "Maybe it's a bird," Amelia said, but she didn't sound sure.

They crept forward, stepping around the roots that stuck up from the ground. Liam's heart was beating fast. The sound came again, clearer now. "Over here." Liam pushed through the overgrown weeds toward a big fallen log. "I think it's—"

He stopped.

Nothing.

Behind the log was just a pile of old leaves.

"There!" Amelia pointed toward the water's edge. But when they got close, it was just a couple of branches clacking together in the wind.

The sound came again. Definitely not the wind. Definitely not a bird.

Liam squinted, scanning the bushes and rocks. He stepped closer to the water, then circled back. "It's coming from over here."

Amelia joined him, pushing aside a curtain of hanging vines. She stepped on a stick.

Crack-POP!

They both jumped. "Ah!" she squealed, grabbing his arm. "Sorry."

Liam looked at her face—how big her eyes were—and couldn't help but laugh. "You about scared me to death.

"You jumped like you got stung by a bee."

"Yeah, well so did you."

They grinned at each other, but then the sound came again, and their smiles faded. Behind the vines was a little hollow made of brush and rocks. It was dark inside. The sound was coming from in there.

Liam dropped to his hands and knees. The ground was damp. Little pebbles pressed into his palms, and a slimy leaf stuck to his thumb. He crawled forward inch by inch.

The sound stopped.

Everything went quiet except for his own breathing.

Amelia gasped. A hand flew to her face.

That's when he saw it too.

5

"HE'S JUST A BABY," Amelia whispered.

Liam leaned closer. The pup was no bigger than a loaf of bread, his patchy fur damp—tan, black, and white with a thin stripe down the middle of his face. Long ears hung over his eyes, and he looked so small and shaky that if you picked him up wrong, he might have just come apart.

When the stray blinked up at them, something tugged in Liam's chest. "Hey there, fella." He crouched. "We ain't gonna hurt you."

The pup whimpered, and a quick pink tongue darted out, licking at his tiny nose.

"Where's his mom?" Amelia asked, glancing around the hollow.

Liam stood, squinting into the thickets and tall grass. He stepped over a root, checked behind a clump of bushes, then kneeled to peer under a log.

Nothing. Not a sign of the pup's mom.

He kept thinking maybe she was watching from somewhere close, waiting for him to leave. But the woods stayed silent, except for a fly buzzing around his ear. "Don't know. Maybe she's out lookin' for food?"

Even as he said it, something sank heavy in his gut.

Too skinny. Too scared.

That pup had probably been alone for days now.

Amelia reached out slowly, letting the puppy sniff her fingers. His tail gave the tiniest wag. "We can't just leave him here," she said, looking at Liam.

He nodded, then scooped him up without a second thought. "Come on, boy. Let's get you someplace safe."

As they headed back through the trees, the little body trembled against Liam's, then tucked his nose into Liam's shirt. The dog was warm in his arms but not heavy, more like carrying a flour sack shirt Ma had just taken off the line.

Amelia kept close, her hand brushing over his droopy ears every few steps. "What should we call him?"

"Don't know yet." Liam looked down at the pup. "What do you think, boy? You look like a ... maybe Rusty?"

"Hmmm." Amelia shook her head. "No, he's not a Rusty. But look at that white stripe and all those spots. What about Patches?"

"Too plain." Liam tilted him for a better look. "See that part? All busted on the edges, like the chips on our dinner plates. Ma's always saying to be careful with 'em."

Amelia's face lit up. "Chip! That's his name!"

"Chip," Liam repeated, nodding. It felt like magic, the way saying a name could make something real. The puppy's ear perked as if he might've heard. "Yeah. That's it."

It was hard to believe he'd just been a scared little creature by the creek. Now he was Chip, and he belonged to somebody—to them.

Amelia suddenly burst into song, making Liam blink.

"Chip the pup with the spot on his nose." She looked over at Liam. "Now your turn."

Huh?

Liam felt prickly all over, like when the pastor called on him in Sunday school and he couldn't recite the verse. He swallowed, wishing she'd sing another line. He gave Chip a little squeeze. Then it just slipped out. "Found him by the creek where the water flows."

"That's good." Amelia said with a smile. Without missing a step, she went on. "Chip the pup, he's brave and true."

"Chip the pup, we'll take care of you," Liam finished, letting out a breath.

"Okay, now let's do it together."

They sang the whole thing again, side by side, their voices tumbling over each other and laughing through the words. Each time they said his name, Chip looked back and forth between them, tail thumping against Liam's arm like he didn't want to miss a thing.

Clouds drifted over the sun as they stepped out of the trees and into the clearing. The shadows were longer now, like the tall posts behind home plate at the ball field, all leaning the same way they were walking. Up ahead, Liam's porch came into view.

Liam jogged up the steps and called through the screen door. "Ma? You home?"

No answer.

He nudged the door open with his elbow, still holding

Chip. "She must've gone into town. Sometimes she walks over to help Mrs. Caldwell snap green beans, and Ma always comes back with a sack full 'cause Mrs. Caldwell says she won't take help for free."

The house felt different with Amelia in it. Smaller somehow. He tried to see it the way she might—how the floorboards creaked louder than they should, how everything looked faded against her bright clean dress. Ma always said their house was plenty good, but standing next to Amelia, Liam wondered if plenty good was the same thing as good enough.

But if Amelia had noticed any of it, she didn't let on. "He needs water," she said. "And food. What've you got?"

Liam set their new friend on the rug by the stove, where he sat wide-eyed and taking it all in. Then Liam grabbed Ma's tin cup, filled it from the pitcher, and set it down. Chip stumbled over, lapping it up so fast that the water splashed the floor.

"Slow down, Chip," Liam said. "Ain't nobody gonna take it from you."

He dug out some leftover cornbread from breakfast and crumbled it into small pieces. Chip dove in with little grunts. When the last crumb disappeared, Chip padded back to the rug and plopped down onto it. Seconds later, he was snoring.

Liam and Amelia sat cross-legged beside him, watching his small chest rise and fall. Chip let out a tiny sigh, one paw twitching like he was already dreaming of better days.

"He's gonna be just fine," Amelia said.

Liam said nothing. He wanted to believe her, but Chip's

ribs were poking against his skin.

What's Ma gonna say about all this? Is she gonna let me keep him?

His thoughts went to the conversation he'd overheard with Mrs. Patterson months back—Ma worrying about enough food for the two of them.

Maybe not.

Liam didn't understand all the words Ma used when she talked about money—like "making ends meet" and "getting by"—but he understood the look on her face when she shook the coffee tin, listening to the coins rattle inside.

Amelia's folks probably never had to do that. With that big house and all those shiny cars, surely they could feed one more mouth.

Part of him liked the idea of Chip in a big yard with a fence and bowls that stayed full. But another part—maybe the bigger part—wanted him right here, close enough to reach out and touch. And Liam had found him too, hadn't he? That had to count for something.

Amelia rested her hands in her lap, her eyes moving from the puppy to Liam. After a moment, she scooted closer. "I wonder if my daddy might let me keep him."

"Why not? Your house is big enough for ten dogs."

Amelia grinned. "That's true ... and I think Mom likes animals." She bunched a bit of her dress in her fist. "Will you come with me to ask? Pretty please? With sugar on top?"

6

"Knew I could count on you." Amelia scooped Chip into her arms before Liam even finished nodding. Out the window, the sun was half gone, making the sky pink and gold, and so bright he almost forgot to move until she darted for the back door and yelled, "Race you there!"

Liam tore after her, laughing between breaths. "Cheatin'—you started first!"

Chip lifted his head, ears flying back like laundry on the line when the wind kicked up. Amelia's braid bounced with each step, and for a few seconds, Liam almost forgot where they were headed.

The field blurred past with grass whipping by and grasshoppers jumping every which way. Liam pumped his legs, but the closer they got to the big house, the tighter his stomach felt. Between breaths, he wondered if the inside would smell like fresh biscuits or like the soap they used at church. In another few strides, the white columns out front got taller and taller until they had arrived at the stone steps. The first one came nearly to his knee.

Liam tipped his head back.

Do folks ever trip trying to climb these?

His palms went damp, and he wiped them on his pants, leaving faint streaks of dust.

Amelia was already halfway up the steps when she looked back and placed a hand on her hip. "Are you coming?"

Maybe?

Part of him wanted to turn around, but he'd already come this far. Why was he so worried? Amelia was nice. Maybe her mom and daddy were too. He hoped so anyway. Releasing a shaky breath, he squared his shoulders and took a step. Then another. By the time he reached the top, Amelia was pushing open the green door that was tall enough to swallow his whole front porch back home.

"Mom?" she hollered.

The moment Liam stepped through behind her, his mouth fell open. The floor was slippery-looking, and his bare feet made no sound on it, unlike the hollow thump they made on the wooden ones back home. He sniffed, pulling in a breath that filled his nose and burned a little.

Lemons. But stronger.

He craned his neck to see the top of the ceiling. Hanging there was a sparkly thing made of a million tiny pieces of glass, like somebody broke a bunch of jars and stuck them back together. On the wall, a big wooden shield had their name—*Jensen*—painted across it, with swirly shapes all around. The wood was shiny where the light from the sparkly thing above hit it. Liam didn't know why anybody would need their name on the wall. At home, the only words hanging up were on the *Homemade Jam 10¢ a Jar* board Ma and Mrs. Patterson would set by the road every so often. To his right, a staircase curved upward, carved with flowers and vines. To his left, he saw a room filled with furniture that looked like it belonged inside a museum. "Whoa."

"Amelia?" A lady's voice floated from somewhere inside. "That you, darling?"

"Yes, Mom! I got a friend with me!"

Footsteps clicked across the floor until Amelia's mom appeared. She was real pretty and had on a necklace made of white marbles, like one of those movie stars at the picture show. Same auburn hair as Amelia too, but hers was pinned up neat, not a strand out of place. Her blue dress looked brand new, with tiny buttons and tall pointy shoes that made a soft tap on the floor. She even smelled nice, like flowers or maybe something clean.

Liam's eyes went to Amelia's scuffed white shoes, then to her mom's spotless ones. His bare toes curled against the floor. He wished he'd thought to wipe the dirt off them.

"This is Liam," Amelia said.

Liam stuffed his hands in his pockets. "Hello, ma'am."

"Well, it's very nice to meet you, Liam." Her smile reached her eyes. Then she looked at the puppy in Amelia's arms. "And who's this little fellow?"

"His name's Chip," Amelia said quickly. "We found him all alone. Can I keep him? Pretty please?"

Amelia's mom came closer, her shoes still making that *click-click* sound. She looked at Chip like Ma looked at peaches to see if they were bruised. Chip squirmed, and Amelia tucked him tighter against her chest. "He's quite small. And rather dirty."

"We found him in the woods. He's just a baby. He needs us."

Heavy footsteps thudded closer. Something slapped down on a table—paper, maybe—and the sound made Liam's shoulders jump. Mrs. Jensen's hand went to her necklace, and even Amelia stood a little straighter. Liam did too.

That's when he saw him.

The dark-haired man was even taller than he'd looked out in the fields. He wore a suit that didn't have a single wrinkle, and his shoes were shiny as new pennies. A gray hat sat tilted on his head, like the men in the newspaper ads. The air around him smelled smoky, like after Mr. Carter from church lit one of his cigars out by the steps. He looked all around, stopping on Mrs. Jensen for a second before looking at Amelia. When he talked, his voice seemed to fill the whole room. "What's all this commotion about?"

Amelia gave Liam a quick smile, then turned toward her daddy. "This is Liam." She lifted the puppy higher. "And this is Chip."

"Hello, Mr. Jensen." Liam tried to sound braver than he felt.

His eyes moved to Liam's bare feet and stayed there for a second before coming back up. Then he gave a quick nod. Liam dropped his eyes to the floor, rubbing the back of his neck. His ears felt hot.

In the silence, Chip let out a yawn.

Mr. Jensen's face didn't change. "I see. And where exactly did this ... Chip ... come from?"

"We found him by the creek. All by himself, Daddy. He

would've died!"

"Amelia, we can't simply—"

"Please, Daddy? I'll take good care of him. Promise!"

Amelia's daddy looked at her mom. Her mom's eyebrows lifted slightly. It was the face grown-ups made when they talked without words.

"The responsibility of a pet is quite significant," Mr. Jensen said slowly. "It requires discipline. Commitment."

"I know, Daddy. I can do it. I know I can."

"What about your piano lessons? You've been less than enthusiastic about them lately."

Liam watched as Amelia's face went through about three different expressions at once. "I'll practice every single day for as long as you want. And I won't complain anymore."

Her mom reached out and touched Chip's head. "He is sweet."

Chip looked up at her and wagged his tail.

Mr. Jensen was quiet for a long time before letting out a big sigh. "Very well. But the moment your piano practice suffers, or the moment this animal becomes a nuisance, he goes. Do I make myself clear?"

"Yes, sir!" Amelia's eyes went wide, like she couldn't believe it. "Oh, thank you, Daddy!" She bounced up and down and pressed her cheek to Chip's fur.

"He needs a bath before he goes anywhere else in this house," her mom said.

Amelia turned to her mom. "Can we give him a bath now?" Then she looked over at Liam. "You can help too."

A bath? In here?

Liam's eyes flicked to Mr. Jensen, and he thought about

what would happen if he dropped a bucket in here—maybe even scratched the floor. He let out a slow breath and stared at a rug so clean it looked like nobody had ever stepped on it. His mouth went dry, and he shook his head. "I gotta go home. Ma's probably wondering where I am."

Amelia frowned. "See you tomorrow?"

Liam scratched Chip's ears. The puppy licked his forearm. "Yeah. Tomorrow."

Amelia's mom walked him to the door. "It was lovely to meet you. You're welcome here anytime."

But as the big green door closed behind him, Liam wasn't so sure.

Walking home felt like it took forever. The air smelled salty and like wet grass after rain. Crickets sang from the fields, following him across the dirt and up to the porch. Up close, the house was just a dark shape against the evening sky. He took the steps two at a time, yanked the screen door open, and let it slam behind him.

"There you are." Ma's voice came from the stove. "I was starting to worry."

"Sorry, Ma. I was with Amelia."

Ma glanced over. "You look funny. What's the matter?"

Liam sat at the kitchen table, the wood all scratched from years of cutting things on it. He sighed as his eyes settled on the shelf by the sink, dishes stacked crooked. At Amelia's, every dish matched and sat neat in a tall cabinet with glass doors, just like in the store in town. "Ma, how come some folks got real nice stuff and we don't?"

Ma paused her stirring and turned, wooden spoon in hand. "What's got you thinking about that?"

He sighed. "Amelia's house is real big, Ma. They got this sparkly thing hanging from the ceiling, and the floor's shiny like nothing I've ever seen. And they all had real nice shoes—brand new lookin'."

Ma nodded. "Sounds like they do have some fancy things over there."

"But why, Ma? How come they get all that good stuff?"

Ma went back to stirring, steam rising all around her face. "Well," she said, "some folks get money from their families. Some work real hard for it. And folks like us, well, we just do our best with what we've got."

"That don't seem fair if you ask me."

"Maybe not. But you know what, sugar? Fancy things don't make you happy. And they sure don't make you a good person."

Liam thought about how Mr. Jensen's eyes had stopped on his bare feet like he'd done something wrong just by standing there. It was strange how one look could make him feel smaller than he'd ever been, even when he was already a boy.

"I know folks with big houses who ain't very nice," Ma said. "And I know folks who don't have much, but they're happy every day."

"What about us?"

Ma smiled, reaching over to ruffle his hair. "Well, I got my boy home safe, and we got beans and cornbread for supper. That makes me feel pretty rich."

Liam leaned back in his chair and looked around their kitchen. It wasn't much, but it smelled like Ma's cooking and the soap she used. It was home. He figured if you could sit in a kitchen that smelled like supper, with someone who loved you, it didn't matter if the house was big or small—you already had the best thing there was.

"Ma?"

"Yeah, son?"

"I love you."

She reached down and cupped his cheek, her palm warm and smelling faintly of flour. "I love you too, sugar. More than all the big houses in the whole world."

7

September 1948

"You excited about school starting?" Ma asked, pinning a shirt to the line.

Liam shrugged. "Guess so."

School meant Tommy Ashford and his gang waiting by the fence, kicking dirt on his shoes and calling him names. Every year, Liam hoped this might be the one that Tommy finally went off to the rich kids' school in Savannah. But Tommy always said his daddy thought it was too far for now, and he liked reminding everybody of it.

It also meant Amelia with her fancy teacher, while he was stuck in Mrs. Finley's room, counting cracks in the wall and staring out the window. Summer had flown by, and all the best parts had gone with it.

At least Chip was doing fine. Amelia's folks had gotten him a collar, and though he had his own bed, Amelia swore he liked sleeping on the rug by the front window the best, where he could see the sun coming up. Chip smelled good all the time too, like wash day, and Liam couldn't help but wonder if the pup got more baths than he did. Still, she brought him over every day, and maybe that part wouldn't change.

After all, Chip had been part of everything that summer, and Liam's mind kept drifting back to the days they'd made their own, days that felt bigger than the whole world ...

⁓ℓℓ⁓

By summer's end, Chip wasn't the same pup they'd found. He'd trailed them through the tobacco rows, down to the creek, and up the old oak tree until he got too scared and whined for them to come back down. He'd even grown some too, but still fit in Liam's lap when they sat under the pecan tree.

One afternoon, Amelia tried to teach him to "shake," but Chip mostly just licked her fingers and wagged his tail. That same day, they'd found a hollow log big enough to crawl through, discovered a patch of wild blackberries that stained their fingers purple, and even built a fort out of feed sacks and sticks behind the tobacco barn. To them, it was a castle, even if the roof sagged and the walls leaned every which way. It was theirs, and that was all that mattered.

Then there was the boat.

They'd found old boards by the barn and dragged them to the creek. Amelia said they could make something "grand" with them. Liam wasn't sure if "grand" was the right word, but by the time they tied the boards together with twine and added a bent piece of tin for a seat, it sure looked like a boat to him.

"You sure it won't sink?" Liam asked, pushing the boat into the creek.

"Only one way to find out."

Amelia grinned and hopped in. The boat wobbled and dipped. Water sloshed in just enough to darken the boards. Liam scrambled in beside her, nearly tipping them both. But it held. On the muddy bank, Chip ran back and forth, whimpering like they were sailing off to China without him.

"Come on, boy!" Liam tapped the tin seat with his hand. "Don't be scared!"

Chip put one paw in, then jerked back. Finally, with a whine, he jumped in, landing with a thud that made the whole thing rock. For a second, Liam thought they were all going in the water. But the boat settled, and they floated down the creek as if they were explorers finding new land. Chip's tail thumped the boards, and the breeze brought the smell of mud and pine. For a while, there was only this moment: no school, no Tommy Ashford, no worry about tomorrow. Just the three of them floating down their own secret piece of the world.

But the best day was when Liam had brought his Pa's old pocketknife to the pecan tree.

"What's that for?" Amelia asked, sitting cross-legged in the shade.

"You'll see."

Liam ran his thumb along the smooth handle, then pressed the blade against the bark. First a circle, followed by a bumpy heart shape around it. His hands shook so much he had to stop twice, wiping the sweat on his pants before getting back to it. The bark had left little ridges on his skin, and the knife felt heavy in his small hands—heavier than when Ma had shown him how to whittle sticks. This was different though. This was forever.

What if Amelia laughed? What if she thought it was silly?

Well, maybe it was. But Ma's voice played in his mind: *Don't quit halfway, Liam. You finish what you start.*

That was enough to keep him going.

Inside the heart, he had carved the letters: *A + L.* The letters weren't even, but when he stepped back, he felt a strange feeling he couldn't name but couldn't let go of either. His Pa had held this knife once, and now it had made something that might last longer than all of them.

Amelia leaned closer to the tree. "What's it mean?"

"Means we'll be friends forever." Liam ran his finger over the rough letters. His face was hot, though he didn't know why.

"Promise?"

He looked at her—really looked—at the sunlight in her hair that made her eyes seem green instead of brown, and at the blue dress she had on, bright as the summer sky. "Promise."

She smiled and traced the heart with her finger. "I like it."

Liam looked at the crooked letters again. It wasn't much, but it was enough to make her smile, and somehow that was everything.

Only one thing left to do.

They spat in their palms and shook the same way the boys did at school when something really mattered.

"Liam, you hear me?" Ma's voice cut through his daydream. "Mrs. Finley wrote. Said she's lookin' forward to seeing you in class again."

He blinked, pulling himself back. "That's good, I guess." Three weeks had passed since the day at the pecan tree. Now, sitting on the porch steps, he wondered why good things had to end.

Ma hummed one of the church songs everybody knew while she bent to gather more pins.

Liam picked at a splinter. "Ma? Think things'll be different this year?"

She paused. "Different how?"

"Just ... different. I don't know."

Ma sat down beside him. "You worried about them boys again?"

He shrugged. "Maybe."

She wrapped an arm around him. "Sugar, I can't promise those boys won't try you. But you're stronger than you think. Smarter too. Don't let anybody make you feel small."

Before Liam could answer, Chip came bounding up the path, followed by Amelia.

"Liam!" she called, her pink dress flying in the wind.

Liam found himself staring. He hadn't seen her in that dress before. The pink made her stand out against the dusty road, and for a second, he thought she looked prettier than anybody he'd ever known.

"Guess what?"

"What?"

"It's my birthday! Remember?"

Liam's stomach sank. "Oh ... yeah. Happy birthday."

"Thank you." She curtsied. "I told you there's a party today. We're having cake and playing games. Aren't you coming?"

When she'd asked last week, he said he'd think about it, but then he just forgot.

A party at the big house. With other kids. Rich kids.

Maybe forgetting hadn't been much of an accident at all.

"I'd like to, but I don't know ..."

"Please?" She made her eyes big, like Chip when he wanted scraps from the table. "It won't be any fun without you."

Ma gave him a little nudge. "That sounds nice, don't it, Liam?"

He glanced at Amelia's hopeful face. "Okay, I'll be there."

"Good!" Amelia clapped. "It starts at two o'clock. Don't be late!"

After Amelia disappeared down the path with Chip, Ma went into the house. When she came back with a damp rag and that look on her face, Liam knew what was coming. She kneeled in front of him and wiped his cheeks. "Be still now." She swiped behind his ear, then his hands.

"Ma ... maybe I shouldn't go."

"Nonsense. Amelia invited you, didn't she?" She brushed at her apron. "Besides, a party's a party. You'll have fun."

Liam didn't answer. He thought of the last time Ma had said something would be fun. The preacher's wife had asked him to stand up front and sing with the other kids. His knees had knocked together, and the words slipped clean out of his head. He remembered everyone staring and Ma giving him that gentle nod like it would help put the words in his mouth. But all he could do was swallow and keep his eyes on the hymnbook until the song was over.

He didn't want another day like that one. Not with Amelia watching, not with all her friends.

Ma must've felt it too. She bent down and went at his shoes with the rag, scrubbing until the brown looked more gray than anything. The scuffs didn't come out, and the hole by his toe still showed. She stopped for a second, as if she might say something, then just tucked the flap under his sock, smoothing it down with her thumb. "There. Nobody'll notice."

eee

That afternoon, with each step he took toward the big house, the knot in his stomach grew tighter. Up ahead, long, colorful ribbons hung from the trees. Shiny cars filled the driveway, even more than at church on Easter Sunday. Kids in clean clothes ran across the grass, hollering to each other. The grass was so short and green it looked like somebody had cut it with scissors. Women in bright dresses and big hats stood out on the porch. He heard their voices and smelled good food coming from the inside.

Liam stopped where the dirt road turned into a yard. The flap at his toe had already worked loose. He pressed his foot down hard, hoping nobody would see. Somewhere a balloon popped, and he flinched.

"Liam!" Amelia came running over. "You made it!" She

grabbed his hand and yanked him toward the house. "Come meet everyone!"

His throat went dry.

What if I say the wrong thing?

These weren't like the kids from school. Every boy had a shirt pressed flat as paper. Every girl had ribbons bright as candy wrappers, and shoes that looked like they might squeak if you touched them.

Liam thought of the patch that pulled at his knee when he walked. He looked down and kicked a twig.

I shouldn't be here.

"This is my friend Liam," Amelia announced to a group of kids by the punch table.

A girl in a yellow dress looked him up and down like she was deciding whether he was worth talking to. Next to her, a boy with a bow tie had pants that fit just right. Liam felt the breeze on his bare ankles and bit his lip.

"Where do you go to school?" the boy asked.

"Hadley Cove Elementary."

The girl in the yellow dress wrinkled her nose. "Isn't that a public school?"

"Yeah, I guess."

"Oh." She turned and whispered something behind her hand to another girl, and they both started giggling.

Liam stuffed his hands in his pockets.

These kids talked different. Somehow, their words sounded better. And they stood different too. Liam wondered if they'd been born knowing how to act this way, or if their parents had made them take lessons for it.

"Let's go see the cake!" Amelia said, pulling him away.

At the table, the cake stood three layers tall with pink roses made of icing and *Happy Birthday Amelia* written in big letters. It rested on a white cloth and was surrounded by presents wrapped in shiny paper.

Liam's eyes widened. "That's the biggest cake I ever saw."

"Mom ordered it from Savannah." Amelia lifted her chin.

Savannah?

Liam had never been, but folks said the stores there had windows taller than a man. Ma once told him a sofa out there cost more than their whole house. Looking at the cake, he figured it probably did too.

For a second, he forgot everything else. The roses looked so real that Liam wanted to reach out to touch one, just to see how it felt. He decided not to and might've kept staring all afternoon, but movement by the punch bowl caught his eye. A couple of boys had stopped whispering. Their heads tilted his way, and everything went too quiet.

Then behind him, a voice rang out clear as the church bell. "Well, well. Look what the cat dragged in."

The cake blurred in front of him. His knees wobbled, and his hands shook in his pockets. Every part of him screamed to run, but his legs wouldn't listen.

He knew that voice.

Please, Lord. Not him.

8

"HEY, POOR BOY. DON'T be rude."

Liam's heart banged so hard it felt like it wanted to break out of his chest. Right away, he tasted it again ...

Dirt filled his mouth. Tommy's knee crushed into his back. A hand shoved his face down. "Eat it, coward's son." The other boys laughed.

His legs felt heavy. His hands damp. He blinked. Once. Twice. Then the music kicked in, horns blasting and clapping sounds that made his ears ring.

Yard. Cake smell. A party—not school.

The sun burned on his neck. Sweat fell down his back.

Breathe. Just breathe.

Then, as if she were standing beside him, Ma's voice came the way it always did: *You're stronger than you think ...*

He held on to her words. Forced his feet to move. Let out a slow breath and turned around.

And there he was.

Tommy Ashford stood in a clean white shirt and bow tie. His eyes went straight to Liam's shoes. "Nice, Wright. Did you fish 'em out of the creek on your way over?"

Liam looked down. The hole seemed bigger than he'd

remembered.

"Leave him alone, Tommy," Amelia said.

"Just kidding." Tommy smirked. "Guess poor boys don't get jokes."

Behind him, a man in a dark suit appeared, with the same nose and slicked-back hair as Tommy. Liam knew right off—it was Tommy's daddy. He'd seen him in town once, leaving the jewelry store with a gold watch in his hand and climbing into a shiny car parked out front. Folks said he sold big boats to rich people, and Tommy never let anyone at school forget it.

"Son." Mr. Ashford's hand clamped down on his shoulder. His voice was low but heavy. "Don't embarrass me."

"Okay, okay." Tommy said, lowering his head.

His daddy's hand slid to the back of his neck. Tommy's shoulders bunched. "What did you say?"

"I mean—yes, sir."

Tommy's face changed, and he looked smaller under his daddy's hand. Not so scary. He had the same look as when Mrs. Finley called you up to the board and you didn't know the answer. Even his voice sounded different. But when Mr. Ashford let go, Tommy's eyes found Liam again.

Liam's stomach knotted.

Say something. Don't let him see you're scared.

"I—I'm gonna check on Chip." Liam turned to go, brushing by Tommy, and that's when he felt it ... too quick to stop.

His feet got tangled.

His knees buckled.

He went flying forward, arms grabbing at air.

No, no, no—Thud!

The table tipped. Liam toppled with it and slammed straight into the cake. Icing burst against him with a wet, sticky splat. Forks spilled all over the grass. Something broke close to his head.

For a moment, he just lay there, face down. A ribbon skimmed his cheek, and he could smell the sweet frosting under him. He pushed on the ground, slipping once before getting his knees under him.

Liam wobbled to his feet and looked at himself. Frosting covered his shirt. Cake streaked down his pants. Grass and crumbs stuck all over. Between his fingers, clumps of icing squished out.

The mess in front of him looked like a cow had run straight through the table and never stopped. The table was on its side. The cake was smashed. Little glass cups were everywhere, some cracked, some broken. White plates were in pieces. Red and gold paper was ripped back from the boxes.

Gasps. Whispers. Someone's laugh—probably Tommy's.

All eyes fell on him, and before he could say anything, footsteps closed in. "Liam!"

Mrs. Jensen looked him up and down, almost sad, before shifting her attention to the wreck around him.

This was it. He was sure of it. Tommy was caught. And maybe—just maybe—school wouldn't feel so hard any-more.

Liam pointed a finger at Tommy. "He tripped me!"

"Did not!" Tommy backed away, hands out. His grin was still there. "He just fell!"

No, no, no. He's doing it again.

Mrs. Jensen glanced between them. Her eyebrows scrunched up as if she were trying to figure out a hard math problem. When her eyes landed on Liam, they stayed a long time. There was something about her face—like she almost believed Liam. Her mouth opened like she might say something, but then she looked at Mr. Ashford instead. Her shoulders dropped, then she turned away and put a gentle hand on Tommy's shoulder.

Huh?

Tommy's grin got wider. He knew he was winning. He always won.

Liam's heart beat so fast it made his whole body shake. His hands tingled. The laughter, the shoves, the mean things Tommy had said about Pa—all of it came rushing back.

"You liar!" The words flew out of him like steam from Ma's kettle. Before his brain could tell his arm to stop, before he could remember Ma's rules about fighting, before he could think about getting in trouble—

His fist was flying.

Crack!

Right on Tommy's nose.

Tommy yelped and stumbled. Blood trickled down to his top lip.

Liam's knuckles hurt, but that didn't matter. For once, somebody had shut Tommy up, and it had been him. He'd done it. Really done it.

Some kids stepped back. Others leaned forward. Somebody whispered, "Gee whiz."

For a blink, he felt bigger, stronger—like the knight in

Amelia's fairy tale book who finally beat the dragon.

Then it hit him. Ma's voice rang in his head: *Fightin' don't solve a thing, sugar. We're better than that.*

But Tommy wasn't better. And now neither was he.

"Liam Wright!" Mrs. Jensen grabbed his wrist. "That's quite enough!"

"But he—"

"I think perhaps it would be best if you went home now," Mrs. Jensen said, leaving no room for arguments.

The words stung harder than a slap.

Liam looked around. Faces everywhere. Amelia's eyes went wide. Tommy held his nose with blood on his fingers. Kids whispered behind their hands. Others tried not to smile.

The heat on his face spread down his neck. He dropped his eyes to the grass and mumbled something—he didn't even know what.

Then he bolted.

He ran past the fancy ladies in their big hats. Their voices followed him:

"What in the world ..."

"Whose boy is that?"

His shoes slapped against the gravel driveway, past the shiny cars, and into the field where the tall grass snagged his pants. The party sounds faded behind him. First the music, then the voices. Soon, all he could hear was his own breathing, hard and fast, and his feet pounding the dirt. His throat burned. His legs felt like rubber. But he kept running until he couldn't hear anything from the big house anymore.

By the time he reached the pecan tree, his legs gave out. He dropped against the trunk, shoulders shaking, and cried until it hurt to breathe.

"Ma said you'd be here, Pa," he whispered. "Said you'd be here whenever I needed you. I wish you could tell me what to do. I wish ..." His voice cracked. "Wish you hadn't gone to that war."

Other kids still had their daddies. Why'd his have to be the one who didn't come back?

"Jack's daddy showed him how to throw a fastball. Charlie's daddy fixed up his wagon good as new. And Billy's daddy showed him how to box. What about me, Pa? Who's gonna help me?"

He waited, like maybe the tree might answer for him. But all it gave him was shade. Maybe that had to be enough for now.

Liam wiped his nose on his arm and stared out across the field toward home. Ma would want to know what happened. What was he gonna tell her? That he fell? That Tommy tripped him? That he ruined everything?

He looked down at his good shirt. Pink icing was smeared across the front, same color as the paint he'd used once when he spent all day helping Mr. Miller fix up candy crates. All he'd gotten for it was a Moon Pie, and he'd eaten that in about three bites.

Could soap fix it?

His head hurt too much to think about it.

Better to stay here. Can't go home. Not yet.

Liam pressed his back against the rough bark and pulled his knees to his chest. It was quiet except for the bugs buzzing nearby. His breath came all jerky, and he kept sniffling.

Then the grass rustled.

He froze. For a second, he was sure it was Tommy, coming to finish what he started. But a black nose poked through first, then Chip's head popped up, tongue hanging out and tail going crazy.

"Hey, boy."

Chip trotted over and licked at the icing on his shoes.

"How'd you find me?" Liam rubbed Chip's ear. Out of the corner of his eye, something moved.

That's when Liam saw her.

"Amelia?" Liam scrambled up fast. "What're you doing here? Your party—"

"Not much of a party now." Amelia stepped through the tall grass, still in her pink dress. "Mom and Daddy are inside talking with Mr. Ashford. He was talking real loud at Daddy. Said he didn't want to do deals with us anymore. Daddy looked awful worried."

Liam's stomach twisted.

Deals?

That sounded big. Grown-up big. He didn't know what deals, but the way Amelia said it made it feel like money or houses. And now it was *his* fault.

"I'm sorry 'bout your cake."

"You didn't ruin anything." She looked at him with serious eyes. "He really tripped you, didn't he?"

Liam nodded. "He's always mean to me at school."

"I believe you," Amelia said. "Told Mom, but nobody listened."

They sat quiet for a minute, watching Chip chase a cricket through the grass.

"I don't think I'm supposed to be friends with kids like you," Liam said finally.

"What do you mean?"

"Kids with big houses, fancy clothes, cakes from Savannah. I don't fit."

Amelia moved closer and grabbed his hand.

Liam stared at their hands pressed together, like it was the strangest and best thing he'd ever seen in his life. He didn't know why holding her hand mattered so much. But it did—more than the cake, more than the party, more than anything. The longer she held on, the warmer he got, like the feeling was crawling up his arm and straight into his chest.

Maybe he didn't fit in at the big house and maybe he never would. But with her hand in his, he finally felt like he belonged.

Before he knew what was happening, she leaned over and pressed her lips to his.

Everything in Liam went perfectly still.

The kiss was soft as a peach and warm as sunshine. He didn't know what to do with his free hand, so he just kept it on his lap. It felt nothing like he'd thought a kiss might. Not like the noisy smacks some kids did at school to tease each other. More like that part at the picture show when Ma made him cover his eyes, but he'd peeked anyway. The man and woman had leaned close, and it looked important, too important to laugh at. That's what this felt like—important.

When Amelia pulled back, her cheeks were pink. "You fit with me."

The words stuck in his head, like they weren't ever gonna leave. His heart thumped so loud he was sure she could hear. He felt he ought to say something big. The kind of words a person would remember forever.

But nothing came. He just stared at her, hoping she somehow knew what he meant. His stomach felt funny—not sick funny, but like there were birds flying around inside. He wanted to touch his lips to see if they felt different, but he didn't want her to think he was being silly.

Amelia glanced down, then back at him. She smiled shy-like. "Can I see you tomorrow?"

He nodded fast. "Yeah. After me and Ma get home from church."

"Pecan tree?"

"Pecan tree."

Chip came bounding back just then, panting, with a leaf stuck to his ear. Liam bent down and kissed the top of his head. "Bye, boy. See you tomorrow."

9

WHERE IS SHE?

Liam kicked at the pecan shells, piling them up only to scatter them again. He did it twice, then a third time, until even that got boring. A grasshopper sprang out when his shoe scraped the shells, then disappeared into the weeds. He brushed his hands on his pants and squinted into the field. A fly buzzed near his ear, and he swatted at it, missing. Every minute felt longer than a Sunday sermon.

The sun kept moving, pulling the tree's shadow across the grass. He picked up another shell, snapped it in half, and let the pieces drop.

Amelia should've been here by now.

She'd told him to meet her, her eyes all serious—the same way they'd looked right before she'd kissed him.

His lips still felt funny from yesterday. Every so often, he'd catch himself touching them, remembering how soft hers had been. Remembering how she'd looked at him after, all shy and pink-cheeked, like they'd shared the biggest secret in the world.

Above him, a mockingbird sang out. Liam watched for a moment, but no other birds answered back. He sighed, drew a line in the dirt, aimed for a weed at the field's edge, and flicked a pebble forward. Missed.

He tried again.

Missed worse.

And still no Amelia.

Liam's stomach grumbled. He should've grabbed a biscuit before he left, but he'd been too excited to even think about food. That felt like hours ago now. Ma had come out once, wiping her hands on her apron. "Don't wait all day, sugar. Maybe that girl plain forgot."

Liam shook his head hard. "She didn't forget."

Ma gave him a soft smile, like she knew better, before going back inside. Liam dug his heels deeper in the dirt.

Maybe she's right.

Maybe the Jensens have fancier church clothes to change into and longer prayers to say.

Maybe her daddy's making her sit at the piano before she can go out.

Maybe her folks are mad about yesterday.

Or maybe they know about the kiss somehow ...

The thought made his chest tight.

Still, Amelia wouldn't just not show up. She'd never done that before, not once. When she said she'd be somewhere, she was there.

The sun climbed higher. His mouth felt dry as dust, but he wasn't going anywhere. A rabbit hopped into the clearing, stared at him for a second, then started nibbling grass.

"Least somebody showed up," he muttered, but the rabbit bolted like he'd shouted.

He leaned back against the tree, tracing the carved heart

with his finger. His eyes grew heavy, and for a while, he must've dozed off, because when he opened them again, the sunlight looked different. The sky was as orange as Ma's peach jam, with purple smudges like blackberry juice dripping on bread.

Ma would be wondering where he was by now. She'd probably saved him some dinner and maybe even a piece of that apple pie Mrs. Patterson had given them at church.

Liam's legs felt twitchy as he paced around the tree, wearing a path in the grass. Every sound made his head snap up: a truck rumbling down the main road, a train whistle blowing, and somewhere far off, a dog barking, but it was too loud to be Chip.

The lightning bugs would be out soon. They'd watched them together every evening all summer. He could see her running barefoot in the grass, hands cupped too tight around a blinking light. "Don't squeeze," he'd told her once. "Or the glow'll quit."

She'd peeked inside anyway, and when the shine faded, her mouth dropped open. Liam had shown her how to cup her palms loose to give the light room to breathe. After that, she'd giggle every time one blinked in her hands, like she'd caught a piece of the night. Sometimes she'd even hold her hands near his face so he could see the tiny glow blink on and off. Her braid would slip over her shoulder as she leaned closer, and somehow her eyes looked brighter than the bug itself. She seemed happier chasing lightning bugs than anybody he'd ever seen.

She wouldn't miss that. Not unless ...

Something was really, really wrong.

For what felt like the thousandth time today, Liam looked toward the big house. He'd never gone there without being invited. Amelia's daddy had made that the rule. So he always waited for her to bring him, to make sure it was okay.

But this was different. This was important.

—⁓—

Liam started walking, but it felt too slow. He broke into a jog, kicking up little puffs of dust with each step. The faster he ran, the sooner he'd get to Amelia.

When the white columns finally came into sight, he sprinted—but halfway down the road, his legs locked up. Something wasn't right. The yard didn't look like it should.

Delivery trucks?

Maybe the Jensens had ordered new furniture. But the men weren't bringing things in—they were taking them out. Boxes, furniture, and stuff Liam didn't even have names for.

"Careful with that!" someone yelled.

Liam flinched, then ducked behind the woodpile, peeking through the gaps between the logs. The front door was wide open.

Four men wrestled Amelia's piano down the steps. One man slipped, and the piano gave a deep *bonk*. Liam's heart jumped. It sounded just like when she'd hit the wrong key, laughed, and kept right on with the Chip song. They'd sung it over and over since the day they'd found him.

Chip the pup, he's brave and true.
Chip the pup, we'll take care of you.

Chip had barked like he was singing too, and Liam had tried to keep the song going, even though his voice cracked. Their sounds had filled the big room until it felt like the three of them had made a world nobody else could touch.

But now strangers were hauling it away, treating it like any old junk. The thought squeezed the air right out of him.

"Hey, boy! You there!"

He jumped. One of the moving men had spotted him—a big fellow with arms like tree trunks.

"You got business here, kid?"

"I'm looking for Amelia. Amelia Jensen." The words came out smaller than he meant.

The man wiped his face with a dirty rag, then shook his head and kept moving.

Somewhere past the trucks, a voice rose above the thumping and scraping. "Liam?"

He turned. Simeon was walking over from where he'd been talking to one of the truck drivers. His clothes were wrinkled and dusty. "What you doing here, son?"

"Looking for Amelia. We were supposed to meet."

Simeon's eyes softened. He glanced back at the house, then at the trucks, then down at his boots. "Come on. Let's walk."

They headed toward the tobacco fields, where the smell was strong and sweet at the same time. Voices floated across the rows. Men were still out there working. The plants looked taller, like they'd grown since yesterday.

Simeon stopped walking and turned to face him. "Mr. Jensen got news last night."

"What kind of news?"

"The kind that makes a man pack up his family in the middle of the night."

"Oh." Liam shoved his hands in his pockets. "They're really gone?"

"Yes. Left before dawn."

Liam's throat tightened. "Was it 'cause I hit Tommy?"

"This was bigger than any boy's fight." Simeon looked down at Liam for a long moment, as if he was deciding something. His mouth opened, then shut. He rubbed the back of his neck and glanced toward the house, where more boxes came out the door. "This was about money, son. Things that don't got a lick to do with you."

Liam swallowed hard. "What about Chip?"

Simeon blinked. "That dog?"

"Yeah. He was ours."

Simeon let out a breath and put a hand on Liam's shoulder. "Life don't ask us what we want, son. That dog went with 'em. But I reckon he'll be looked after. Best thing you can do now is remember the good you gave him while he was here."

Liam saw Chip in his mind—ears flapping, tumbling through the fields, chasing grasshoppers till he dropped, curling up between him and Amelia under the pecan tree. He saw the day he and Amelia had found him. For a moment, the memories felt close enough to grab. Then they slipped away, just as quick as Amelia and Chip had.

His nose burned, and his eyes went watery, like looking through creek water. He swiped at them with his sleeve.

Simeon patted Liam's back—not soft like Ma when he had a bad dream, but slow and steady all the same—then started toward the house.

Liam watched him take a few steps, then called out. "Simeon?" His voice came out thin, like it didn't want to come out at all.

Simeon turned. "Yeah, son?"

"You think I'll ever see 'em again?"

10

May 1960

SAWDUST DRIFTED THROUGH THE sunlight cutting across the frame. The air smelled of cut pine and hot tar from the shingles.

"Pass me that level," Simeon called from nearby.

Liam tossed it over and watched the older man set it against the beam.

"Give it a few more weeks and you'll be moving in," Jerome said with that easy smile of his that made the work feel lighter.

"Y'all don't have to give up your Sundays for this."

"Your ma fed us plenty at the farm. Least we can do is help her boy get back on his feet." Jerome grinned, reaching for a hammer. "Remember when your ma brought that big pot of stew out to the farm? Fed us so good we passed out in the shade until Simeon came yelling at us."

Simeon poked his head around the corner. "Should've known better than to let y'all eat first. But I'd have done the same thing with stew that good. Your ma was a good woman."

Liam's mouth twitched, then faltered. He turned away.

The ache of missing her—and the old farm—still pressed in, though three years had passed. Even now, no matter how broad his shoulders had gotten, some folks still looked at him like the boy who'd lost everything in one night. Jerome and Simeon meant well, but their kindness sometimes felt like a reminder of what he used to be instead of who he'd become.

A low putter rose on the dirt road before the thought could settle. An old Ford pulled up, dust billowing behind it, and out stepped the driver with a basket in hand and her Sunday hat tilted against the sun.

The smell reached them first—biscuits and something sweet underneath.

The men dropped their tools as quickly as boys called to supper.

"Now don't go thinkin' this is for you lazy lot," Mrs. Patterson called, walking up the path. "I baked for the church ladies, and you just happen to be on my way."

Jerome laughed, already wiping his hands on his shirt. "Then I reckon we'll take the burden right off you."

Simeon shook his head, grinning. "Didn't know I was gonna eat twice this morning. Would've worked twice as hard if I'd known."

"You boys work hard enough." Mrs. Patterson set the basket down on a plank and lifted the cloth. She handed Liam a plate with a biscuit, spooned gravy over it, and finished the plate with a wedge of pie. "How's the room above Miller's treating you?"

He shrugged. "Fine. Quiet most nights."

She gave Liam the look that always meant she still wished he'd take the spare room at her place. They'd danced this dance a dozen times: she offered, he declined, and nothing changed.

Maybe it was pride. Maybe it was just the stubbornness of being twenty. Either way, something in him needed to make his own way. Even if it meant eating beans from a can and reading by lamplight in a room hardly bigger than a closet.

Next, Mrs. Patterson fixed a plate for Jerome, swatting at his hand when he tried to sneak a bite before she was done. Then she piled Simeon's just as high and looked back at Liam. "Job at the boatyard still suiting you?"

"Can't complain. Pay's good enough to buy all this lumber," Liam said.

She nodded. "I know it puts bread on near every table in Hadley Cove these days. Man does what he has to." She lowered her voice. "Doesn't mean I have to like who signs the checks."

"We all punch that clock same as Liam," Jerome said with a half-laugh. "Don't mean we like it either."

"He's right." Simeon tapped his fork against the empty plate, chasing the last crumbs. "Money's money."

Liam tore off a piece of biscuit, dragged it through the last streak of gravy on his plate, and popped it in his mouth. "Mr. Ashford mostly leaves us be."

"It's his boy I'd worry about. For all of you."

Tommy Ashford.

Liam hadn't thought about him in a long while. Last he'd

heard, Tommy was off at college, learning whatever it was rich boys learned when they weren't busy making life miserable for others.

"That's ancient history," Liam said. "We were just kids."

He told himself it didn't matter anymore. But before he knew it, he was back in the schoolyard, watching Tommy snatch the brown paper sack from his hands and shake out the contents—cold beans wrapped in wax paper. Tommy had held it high. "Look here—poor boy's feast," he'd snickered, before tossing it in the dirt and grinding it under his heel. The beans had seeped into the ground, and Liam's stomach had growled until supper.

That was the last year before Tommy left for the private school in Savannah.

Liam blinked and looked down at his plate. Only crumbs remained. Jerome and Simeon were talking about something—their voices reached him, but the words didn't stick. He sighed and forced himself to listen.

After the men finished eating and got back to work, Mrs. Patterson pulled Liam aside. She reached into her basket and came out with a book. "Thought you might like this one."

"What's it about?"

"A boy and his fawn. Hard story, but worth it." She placed it in his hands. "Might do you some good."

A boy and his fawn?

The book felt heavier than it looked. He couldn't help but think of Chip as he turned it and read the cover. *The Yearling.* He'd never heard of it, but if she was handing it to him, there was a reason.

Over the past three years, Liam had read whatever he could get his hands on—newspapers, magazines, books folks left behind at Miller's. He thought that was maybe why Mrs. Patterson had started bringing him her collection of novels.

"Your ma always said you were sharp as a tack," she'd told him once. "Don't let hard times keep you from using that brain."

So he read at night in his little room, during lunch breaks at the yard, or just whenever he had a few minutes. Stories of places he'd never seen, of people with troubles larger than his own. Somehow, they made him feel less alone.

"Thanks." He tucked the book under his arm. "I'll bring it back to you when I'm done."

Work went on until the light faded. By evening, the last truck rumbled away, leaving Liam standing alone, staring at what they'd built.

Fourteen twenty-two Muscadine Drive.

Same address where he'd grown up. Same ground where Ma had once cooled pies on the windowsill and where her blue ribbon from the Hadley Cove Fair had once hung above the kitchen doorway. He remembered that day clear as anything ...

———

Ma stood beneath the striped tent with flour still on her apron as the judges awarded her the ribbon for her famous peach pie. Folks clapped and hollered, and she blushed so deeply you'd have thought she'd been out in the sun all afternoon. Mrs. Murphy from down the road hugged her in good-natured defeat, and Mr. Curtis tipped his hat like Ma was royalty.

Liam had been so proud he could barely stand still, watching Ma accept congratulations from what felt like half the county. That's when he'd snuck around to the back of the tent where the leftover pies sat cooling. He'd cut himself two slices and was mid-bite when Ma's shadow fell across him. Peach juice ran down his chin as he scrambled to wipe it with his sleeve.

Too late.

Ma set the whole pie dish in front of him and shook her head. Then she broke out into a smile. "Go on then," she said, laughing. "If you're gonna steal pie, best do it proper. Eat the whole thing."

———ele———

A gust rattled the green shutters he'd painted the day before, snapping him back. Liam's eyes swept over the house. This one would be different. Stronger. Built to last through whatever storms might come. But as he looked at it now, nearly finished, Liam wished Ma could see her boy rebuilding on the same ground where she'd once made life feel whole.

He stood there a moment longer, letting his gaze trace the roofline and the porch steps waiting for railings. For the first time, the place felt less like a worksite and more like a home.

Only then did he cross the threshold. His hand brushed

the frame as if testing its strength. Inside, his boots thudded on the new floorboards. Against the far wall sat the old mantelpiece from Ma's house, one of the few things that had survived Hurricane Ruth. On top of it lay a piece of wood about the size of a small dinner plate. The carving was worn, but the heart and the letters inside were still there: *A + L.*

The last time he'd seen her came rushing back ...

Amelia in her pink party dress.

Chip's wet nose. Tail wagging.

Her warm hand in his. A kiss. The kiss.

Her words: "You fit with me."

Then his lips on Chip's head. "Bye, boy. See you tomorrow."

The pecan tree. Tomorrow.

The memory hit hard, then slipped away. Liam reached out and ran his thumb over the grooves of the initials, feeling every ridge and hollow he'd carved with such care as if that could keep her close a moment longer. Twelve years since he'd carved it with Pa's old knife. Back then, he believed promises lasted forever.

Now he knew better.

11

"Almost there," Liam muttered, lowering the cypress beam. The weight dragged at his shoulders. Rough grain bit into his palms. He eased it toward the clamp, sweat stinging his eyes.

The beam slipped.

Iron jaws snapped as his finger plunged toward them.

He yanked his hand back just in time and caught the beam.

"Got it," Jerome said, securing his end.

Liam steadied it against the hull they'd been shaping all week, then slowly released his grip. "Close one." His hands were shaking. He dragged them down his pants and stepped back.

Around them, hammers cracked against wood. Men called out measurements. The sharp scent of pine shavings tangled with salt air, and heat rose from the planks like the breath of something alive.

Liam's eyes still burned from a sleepless night. Mrs. Patterson's book had kept him up past dawn. He'd promised himself he'd stop after the first chapter. Then the second. By the time the lamp burned low, he was halfway through, and when morning light slipped through the window, he was still turning pages.

"Wright!"

He looked up.

Mr. Ashford picked his way between lumber stacks and coiled rope, dressed more for Sunday service than a boatyard in his pressed shirt, tie, and dark trousers.

"Yes, sir?" Liam rubbed his eyes.

Mr. Ashford stopped and ran his hand along the boat frame. "Fine work."

"Thank you, sir."

"Walk with me a minute."

Liam glanced at Jerome, who raised his eyebrows slightly and then turned back to the beam and busied himself.

Liam's mind raced as he followed Mr. Ashford.

Is this about being late last Tuesday?

Or maybe someone had seen him and Jerome sitting around Thursday afternoon when they'd finished early and were waiting for the new lumber shipment. They'd had nothing else to do, but it probably hadn't looked good.

He was still turning it over in his head when they reached the office, a brick building that sat apart from the dock area. Inside, it was cooler, but not by much. Mr. Ashford's desk was covered with invoices, boat plans, and letters stamped with official-looking letterheads.

"Have a seat." Mr. Ashford settled into his chair and leaned back.

Liam sat stiffly, waiting. No point in guessing now. He'd find out soon enough. There were only two outcomes when Mr. Ashford called you into the office: really good news or really bad.

"I've got a forty-footer starting this week. I need somebody to run the whole build from start to finish. Keep the crew on track and make sure we deliver on time." Mr. Ashford tapped his pencil against the desk. "I want you on it."

"Me?"

"Crew chief. Fifty cents more an hour, plus a bonus when we finish."

Huh?

Liam's fingers tightened on the chair arms. That was nearly half of what he made now. It'd be enough for new boots, maybe a decent chair for the new house, and maybe even a savings jar. He couldn't believe it.

"Been watching you work, Wright. You know boats, know wood. And the other fellas listen when you talk."

"Why not Jerome? Or Simeon? They started before me."

"Jerome's good with his hands, but he doesn't want to tell other folks what to do. And Simeon ..." Mr. Ashford paused. "We both know he's slowing down. Still the best craftsman we've got, but this job needs somebody who can be here every day, without his back giving out."

It made sense. Simeon hadn't been the same since the farm was torn apart. Lately, he had been taking more breaks and picking up shorter shifts. Boatyard work asked different things of a man, like longer hours on his feet and bending over beams heavier than anything a mule ever pulled.

"Truth is, I'm getting too old to run it all myself. Been thinking about bringing in a foreman. You'll have to report to him." Mr. Ashford pulled out his pocket watch. "I'll be traveling to Atlanta a lot over the next few months. Got some supply contracts I'm chasing. Could keep us busy for years if I land them."

"How long you think you'll be gone?"

He shrugged. "Week, maybe ten days at a time. That's why I need good people running things here. Folks I can trust."

The weight of it settled on Liam's shoulders. More responsibility meant more ways to mess up. But it was also more money than he'd ever been offered.

"I'll take it."

"Good." Mr. Ashford scribbled a note. "You'll start Wednesday."

"Yes, sir."

Walking back across the yard, Liam felt different somehow. Crew chief. His own project.

Real money.

The little boy who'd once ducked his head when the Ashfords' car rolled past would've never believed he'd see the day he'd be promoted by Mr. Ashford himself. Time had a way of making the impossible ordinary. The thought made his chest swell, but ache too, remembering all it had taken to get here.

Jerome was waiting at their workstation, and from the look on his face, he'd already heard the news. "Well, look who's moving up in Hadley Cove."

"How'd you hear?"

"Everybody knew. Just a matter of time." Jerome clapped him on the back. "You earned it."

"Where's Simeon? I oughta tell him."

"He left."

"Where'd he go?"

"Don't tell me you forgot. You know what today is."

By sundown, folks had gathered at the docks. Strings of lights ran between the pilings, their glow rippling across the dark water. Tables made from sawhorses and plywood held platters of hush puppies, and corn still steaming in the husks. Jerome had brought his fiddle, and a kid nobody really knew was plucking away at his guitar.

The whole setup felt just right for Simeon's sixtieth birthday party.

Liam grabbed a plate and a beer, then found a spot where he could watch the old man. Simeon's laugh rolled over the music. He'd probably already downed more drinks than his wife approved of. She stayed close by anyway, shaking her head at his stories but smiling all the same.

"Look at him go." Jerome appeared beside him with his beer. "Ain't seen him this happy since his grandson cracked that double at the county game."

"He's earned it."

"Darn right." Jerome took a long gulp from his bottle. "You remember after the hurricane? Ain't no man like him."

Liam was there again ...

Ma's old house, roof half gone, windows shattered. He searched the wreckage, shouting her name. Then found her pinned beneath the beam that had held their roof up since his Pa had built it. She was still breathing when he reached her, but barely. He held her there, whispering how everything was going to be okay. For a moment, he thought she might be gone—until the smallest tremor passed her lips.

"I love you, sugar."

"I love you too, Ma." His hand shook as he smoothed the damp hair from her forehead.

Her eyes fluttered half-open. "Will you do one thing for me?"

"Yes, Ma, anything."

Her breath shuddered. "Don't ever forget: you're stronger than you think."

Liam pressed his face against hers, shutting out the ruin around them, trying to hold on to anything that was still hers. His cheek sank into her hair, and there it was. Through it all, her hair still carried a trace of lavender soap. It was the last thing of her he ever breathed in. He kept rocking her long after, like she used to do with him when he had nightmares, until Simeon's hands pulled him away.

That's when he broke—collapsing into Simeon, choking out the words over and over. "I should've been here."

Simeon pulled him closer. "Son, there's nothing nobody could've done. Nothing."

But Simeon didn't stop there. He was the one who gathered the men, found a preacher, and helped set Ma's coffin in the ground. He told Liam it wasn't much, but it was all they could do.

After that, he kept showing up. For months, clearing debris, and not once asking for thanks. When the place was as picked up as it could be, he went one step further and got Liam and the rest of the farmhands new work at the boatyard. Even when it seemed like the entire town had been washed away, Simeon made sure he and the boys weren't left behind.

—*eee*—

The sounds rushed back—music, laughter. Liam blinked hard and drew a sharp breath, as though he'd surfaced from underwater. "Good man."

"Best we got." Jerome raised his bottle.

Liam lifted his own. "Here's to the old man lasting another sixty."

Mrs. Patterson came bustling over, balancing a three-layer cake with candles that flickered in the breeze off the water. "Y'all get his attention. Time for the song."

Jerome whistled between his teeth. "Hey! Everybody in! Time to embarrass the birthday boy!"

People drifted over from the boats and tables, kids abandoning whatever they'd been doing in the shallows. Mrs. Patterson moved carefully across the uneven planks, protecting those candles as if her life depended on it.

The singing was loud and off-key, but cheerful. Simeon threw back his head, grinning wide. When they got to his name, half the crowd hollered it while the others mumbled through whatever version they remembered.

"Make a wish!" his wife called.

Simeon closed his eyes, then leaned in and blew. Most of the candles went out on the first try. The stubborn ones took another round. Everyone hooted and clapped.

While cake was being served, Liam worked his way over to Simeon.

"There's my boy!" Simeon wrapped an arm around him. "You having a good time?"

"Best party I've been to in years. Got something to tell you, though."

"Yeah? What's that?"

"Mr. Ashford made me crew chief."

For a beat, Simeon just stared. Then he let out a whoop that could've been heard all the way to Savannah. "Well, I'll be! Crew chief!" He scooped Liam into a hug that lifted him clean off the dock. "Boy, your ma'd be proud right now."

The mention of Ma brought the old ache, but warmth too. "Guess that means I'll be giving you orders now."

"You been doing that for years anyway. Now you'll just get paid for it." Simeon slapped his back and walked off.

Mrs. Patterson appeared. Her eyes were bright and watery. She reached up, cupping his cheek. "That's wonderful, honey. Just wonderful."

"Thank you. For everything."

"You're family, Liam. You know that." Her hand moved down and squeezed his arm. "Your ma's watching over you. I know she is. She'd be proud. Proud as I am right now, that's for sure."

Liam tried to answer, but his throat locked up. He only managed a nod.

Mrs. Patterson smoothed the collar of his shirt, the way Ma used to before church. "Now, that's enough of me carrying on. You believe I had to stop one of these men from carving the cake with his pocketknife? Lord help us." She sniffled, shook her head with a half-smile, and hurried back toward the dessert table.

Liam smiled, letting it all soak in. Friends and neighbors, salt air mixing with pipe smoke, kids splashing while their parents talked and laughed. Something from last night's reading came back to him—how life could be fine and beautiful, but never easy.

Life sure hadn't been easy for him, not one bit. But maybe that was what made moments like this matter. People who cared about him, steady work, and this night on the water. Love, he had learned, wasn't just about having enough—it was about making room in your heart even when your hands were already full. People like Mrs. Patterson and Simeon had shown him that.

The music picked up, and couples started dancing on the dock. Boots and bare feet tapped against the planks. Kids darted by people's legs. Swaying lanterns shifted light across faces he'd known for years. Someone clapped along with Jerome's fiddle, and a burst of laughter followed. It struck him how rare it was to see everyone this happy at once. He'd spent so many years feeling like he was on the outside looking in, but tonight felt different. Tonight he belonged. He carried that warmth with him toward the edge of the crowd. Then, cutting through it all, came a sound that reached straight into his chest and grabbed hold.

A bark.

Closer now.

Where the road meets the docks.

Liam's pulse quickened as he pushed through the crowd,

not caring who he bumped into. Beyond the lights, a shadow stood low. The figure shifted. A shape eased forward—hesitant at first, then sure.

Four legs.

Their eyes met.

Another bark.

Closer.

Tan, black, and white—patches shifting in and out of the dock lights.

A step nearer, and long ears came into view, hanging over a graying muzzle.

Another step.

A white stripe down the snout.

Liam's legs wobbled beneath him, his heart thudding so hard it hurt.

It couldn't be ...

12

"Chip?"

The dog's tail whipped wildly as he barreled forward, paws skidding across the dock before springing straight at Liam.

"My boy!" Liam dropped to his knees. Chip pushed against him, whining as if he couldn't get close enough. His fur was softer now, with more gray than brown. The white stripe down his nose had spread wider, and his eyes had gone cloudy the way old dogs' eyes do. But it was *him*.

Chip licked his face with the same enthusiasm he'd had as a pup. "I missed you too," Liam whispered.

Around them, laughter and music continued, but it all dulled into the background. When Liam buried his face into Chip's neck, nothing else existed; just a boy and his dog finding each other again. He could have stayed like that forever. But then he heard it.

Click. Click. Click.

The sound of heels on the dock grew closer.

Click. Click. Click.

The footsteps stopped right in front of him.

"Chip?" a woman's voice called out.

How in the world—

A rush of heat surged through Liam. His pulse kicked up. Slowly, he lifted his head.

The woman's auburn hair was cut short. Pearls glimmered at her ears. Her lips were painted cherry red, and her blue dress caught the light in such a way that it didn't belong to this place. But it was her brown eyes, locking onto his, that stole his breath.

Neither of them moved as if the slightest shift might break whatever held them there. In her eyes, he saw his favorite summer—pecan shells, lightning bugs, and nights under the stars. For a moment, he wasn't a man on a dock but a boy again, staring at the only girl who'd ever really seen him.

She blinked once, and her lips parted. He thought she might say his name. But then—

Car doors slammed.

They both turned toward the sound. Three silhouettes emerged from the road, stepping onto the dock and heading right for them. Liam squinted. A man, a woman, and ...

Mr. Ashford? This late?

The man never stayed a minute past quitting time. Most days, his car was pulling away before the rest of them even had their tools cleaned.

Liam stayed still, his hand resting on Chip's back, watching as the outlines of the man and woman came into focus with every step.

Beside him, the woman straightened, smoothing her dress. Her hands fell to her sides, and she released a quiet sigh. "I should ..." she murmured, but her voice trailed off as the figures drew nearer.

The well-dressed couple stopped a few feet away, taking in the scene. Mr. Ashford hurried past them and pointed behind Liam. "What's all that?"

"Simeon turned sixty," Liam said.

"Right, right." Mr. Ashford waved his hand. "Well, since you're here, there's some important people I want you to meet."

Liam stood. His heart thudded so hard it hurt. The tall man wore a dark gray suit with sharp creases. His silver hair was combed straight back. A cigar smoldered between his fingers, and smoke trailed up past his face. Beside him, the woman's auburn hair was swept up neatly, threaded with streaks of silver at the temples. Her navy dress shimmered with small sequins. A string of pearls hung around her neck, and she carried a small black purse in her gloved hands.

"Mr. and Mrs. Jensen, this is the crew chief I mentioned." Mr. Ashford gestured between them.

What are they doing here?

"This is the man leading your build." He clapped a hand against Liam's shoulder and smiled. "We'll be starting your yacht on Wednesday."

Mr. Jensen gave a brief nod.

Yacht?

Liam returned the nod and rubbed the back of his neck. He'd built big boats before, sure. But a yacht? For the Jensens? For the very people who'd broken his heart in more ways than he cared to remember?

Mr. Jensen studied him. His attention stayed on Liam's face, then dropped to his hands, his clothes, then climbed back to his face. For a second, Liam wondered if something clicked. But then, Mr. Jensen just checked his watch. "We should let you get back to your evening."

Mrs. Jensen turned to Mr. Ashford. "Thanks for meeting us."

"Always glad to have the Jensens in town." Mr. Ashford looked at the woman by Liam. "And good to see you too, Amelia."

"You too, Mr. Ashford," Amelia said.

Liam's stomach fluttered.

Amelia.

The sound of her name pulled him back in time. Suddenly, he was under the pecan tree again, her braid slipping over her shoulder. Her laughter echoing through the dark as they chased lightning bugs. The cool creek water on their ankles, the sun setting slow. He felt the weight of his father's pocketknife in his small hands as he carved their initials into the tree. How serious she'd looked when she asked what it meant. How his chest had swelled when they'd promised they'd be friends forever. And how he'd kept that promise the best he could.

The memory dissolved as the Jensens started toward the road. Amelia's eyes drifted to the dog still pressed against Liam's leg. "Come on, Chip." The dog tilted his head, then took one tentative step toward Amelia, then another. His tail gave a small, uncertain wag before he trotted to her side.

Their voices trailed behind them as they walked away. Liam's gaze followed Amelia between her parents. She glanced back once, and in her face, he thought he saw something he couldn't quite read. Maybe a flicker of what they used to be?

Even so, she hadn't said much. This wasn't all on her though. He could've said something too. So why hadn't he?

Twelve years of wondering what he'd say if he ever saw her again, and when the opportunity came, he'd crumbled. This wasn't the reunion he'd dreamed of a thousand times. He'd pictured her smiling, maybe even glad to see him. Instead, she'd walked away as if he were a stranger.

And she'd taken Chip too, as though Liam had never been part of his life at all. But he was *their* dog. The pup they'd found together, named together, and loved together. The dog who used to sleep next to him under the pecan tree, who'd raced them through tobacco fields and splashed in the creek in times that had felt endless, yet had ended all the same.

Maybe those summer days didn't mean to her what they'd meant to him. Maybe she'd forgotten about the boy who'd carved their initials into the tree, who'd kissed her when she was eight years old, back when the world was simple. Or maybe seeing him reminded her of everything she'd rather forget—the poor boy who didn't belong in her world then and sure didn't belong in it now. Losing someone once was hard enough. Losing them twice ... That was a thought he couldn't bear to linger on.

At least Mr. and Mrs. Jensen hadn't recognized him. They'd looked right past him. Strangely, there was something to be grateful for in that. No awkward questions about the birthday party, or what he'd done with his life, or if he still lived in the same house. To them, he was nobody. And maybe that was better than being somebody they had never truly welcomed.

Once their taillights disappeared, Mr. Ashford cleared his throat. "Wright, this build has to be perfect. Rest up tomorrow; you'll need it. I'll see you Wednesday bright and early."

"Yes, sir."

13

"Ma!" Liam clawed at *the wreckage.*

Splinters dug under his nails.

"Where are you? Ma!"

Her blue ribbon. Kitchen table in pieces.

"Please!" His voice cracked. "Ma!"

More debris. Piled up higher than he could—

"MA!"

The scream tore from his throat as he jolted awake. His heart thudded like it might burst. Sweat cooled his skin as the little room above Miller's store sharpened into focus: wooden walls, a single window, the bed he barely fit on.

Not the hurricane.

He sat up and wiped his face with shaky hands. Same nightmare every time. Always too late.

The night Hurricane Ruth hit Hadley Cove, Liam had been two hundred miles away in Valdosta, helping fix a burned-down barn. Three days' work brought nine dollars cash in his pocket. At seventeen, it had felt like a fortune.

Ma had kissed his cheek before he'd left. "Be careful, sugar. Wind's got a mean sound tonight."

"It'll be fine, Ma. I'll see you Sunday."

But it hadn't been fine. By the time he'd come back, everything was gone.

Liam swung his legs out of bed, splashed water on his face from the basin, and stared into the cracked mirror. The water carried its usual iron smell as it dripped down his chin.

He'd spent his whole life chasing money, doing whatever he could to make things easier for Ma. But what was the point now? He'd worked himself half to death trying to get ahead, and still he'd leave this world empty-handed.

Ma had done the same, working more jobs than he could count. And for what? A house that blew away in one night? A son who hadn't been there when she'd needed him most?

Maybe that was just how life worked.

Liam sighed and then put on his work clothes like every morning before it: wash up, get dressed, and head out to whatever job was waiting. Today, that meant finishing the house he'd been rebuilding since the hurricane.

But this work was different. Nobody was forcing him. Sure, it would've been smarter to save the money and keep the room above Miller's. But something inside him needed to rebuild this house—for Ma, maybe even for Pa. Perhaps what mattered most was building something that lasted, on ground that meant something.

He grabbed his keys and headed downstairs. Inside the store, the bell jingled as a woman entered with two kids. The younger one tugged at her skirt, tattling on his brother.

"Morning." Mr. Miller didn't look up from the mail. "Rent's due tomorrow."

"Yes, sir."

"Coffee's hot if you want some."

"Thanks."

Liam poured himself a cup and peered out the window as the town came alive. Men hurried to work, kids shuffled to school, women carried cloth sacks. Life moved steadily, as if the hurricane had never touched this place. Nothing had really changed. Folks just kept going, probably just hoping today might turn out better than yesterday.

At the counter, Mr. Miller rang up the woman's bread while her kids argued over Pixy Stix. They were new in town, and lately it seemed like every kid wanted them.

Liam sipped his coffee. He was thankful for the roof and bed upstairs. Rent had come cheaper because Mrs. Patterson knew Mr. Miller's wife from church and had spoken up for him. Still, this had never felt like a place he could truly call home.

He set his cup down. "I'll be at the house."

Mr. Miller only nodded, already onto the next customer.

Outside, the morning air was cool. Dew sparkled on the grass, and a thin mist hung low. Around back, his truck waited under the oak. The Meadow Green Ford F1 had more rust than paint when he'd gotten it. He'd spent hours bringing it back to life: fresh paint, polished chrome, and an engine tuned until it purred like it had just come off the line.

When Liam's fingers found the door handle, he paused ...

———

Two weeks after they buried Ma, Liam sat on a stack of flat fieldstones that used to prop up the house. The air still reeked of salt and mildew. Around him lay broken, water-logged wood scattered with debris: a rusty can, a tin pot, a piece of beige fabric that might've been from Ma's dress. He'd been coming here every day, not sure why. There was nothing left to see.

The sound of an engine made him look up. It was Mrs. Patterson's old Buick, but she wasn't alone. Behind her, a truck rumbled to a stop. Meadow green, dented bumper, and one headlight dimmer than the other.

Mrs. Patterson got out slowly, keys jangling in her hand. When she turned toward him, tears were tracking down her cheeks. "Your ma saved for this truck for five years," she said. "Planned to give it to you on your eighteenth birthday."

Liam stared at the Ford. "She never said anything."

Mrs. Patterson sat beside him and pressed the keys into his palm, closing his fingers around them with her own. "She always thought of you first, that woman. Took extra shifts at the cannery, skipped meals she shouldn't have." Her voice wavered. "She'd want you in it, Liam. She'd want you moving forward."

He tightened his grip on the keys and felt something he hadn't felt since the storm. Maybe there was still a tomorrow worth getting to.

The memory faded, leaving only the weight of the keys in his hand. He opened the door, slid in, and turned the ignition. The engine caught on the second try and settled into its familiar rumble. As he pulled out, he rolled down the windows, letting the morning air fill the cab.

The drive took him down Main Street. On the right sat Henry's Hardware, where Ma would sometimes ask if they had any bent nails or screws she could have to fix whatever had broken that week. On the left, the barbershop's red and white pole still spun in circles. Liam had gone there once before a date, and they'd clipped him so unevenly he wore a hat for two weeks. Safe to say, he never went back.

Farther down was Sal's Ice Cream Parlor. He could still see Ma standing with her own chipped bowl, asking if they could get a scoop without paying for the cone. The man had smiled kindly and said, "Of course." He even gave her an extra scoop. Other kids got sugar cones, waffle cones, and some got banana splits. Liam got vanilla in Ma's bowl—and he told himself it tasted better that way.

At the end of Main Street rose the white steeple of the church Ma had dragged him to every Sunday. Nearby stood the brick schoolhouse where Tommy Ashford used to make his life miserable. At the corner, he turned right, passing the overgrown road that led to the old Jensen farm.

The truck bounced along the dirt lane, kicking up dust behind it. From the trees, a cardinal's whistle carried across the fields as fourteen twenty-two Muscadine Drive came into view. The brown wooden boards gleamed in the morning sun, green shutters framed every window, and the wide front porch faced east to catch the sunrise. The house looked almost ready—better than the original, if he was honest. Ma would've been proud of the craftsmanship, even if she'd have scolded him for the expense. He smiled as he turned into the drive.

Then he saw it.

His foot slammed the brake. Dust swirled.

His pulse spiked, hands squeezing the wheel.

Who's that?

14

LIAM FROZE. A BLACK Lincoln sat where his truck should've been.

He couldn't make out the exact model, but it looked like one of those new Continentals he and Simeon had gawked at outside the gas station in Savannah.

Nobody around here drove a car like that. Most folks were lucky to have one at all.

His stomach twisted as he killed the engine and climbed out. He stood there for a beat, wondering if he was in trouble.

The bank?

Maybe he'd slipped behind on a payment, or missed some paper that needed signing. The knot in his gut pulled tighter.

Doesn't make sense.

Susan at the bank would've told him straight when he cashed his check last week.

He let out a slow breath and started forward. When he reached the car, he stopped.

Empty.

He bent down, cupped his hands against the glass, and

peered in. A purse, heels, gloves—women's things left behind.

A prickle ran up his neck. He stepped back, and his eyes moved from the car to the house.

Inside?

He climbed the porch steps and tried the knob.

Locked.

That didn't surprise him. Ma had drilled that into him since he was a boy: *Always lock your doors, sugar. World's full of folks who'll take what isn't theirs.*

Still, he had to be sure. Key in hand, he unlocked the door and pushed it open. "Hello?"

Liam's voice bounced through the empty rooms. No answer. Just the smell of wood and paint. He locked the front door behind him and walked through, checking the front room, the kitchen, and the bedrooms.

Nobody.

He moved back through the kitchen to the back door and tried that too.

Locked.

Liam unlatched it and stepped outside. Grass brushed his boots as he searched the perimeter, checking windows, checking corners. His hammer still lay on the sawhorse where he'd dropped it. The extra boards sat covered with a tarp. A bucket of nails and scraps rested in the dirt in the same untidy pile he'd left Sunday. Nothing touched. Nothing out of place. Everything just as it should have been.

Still, someone had to be here. That car hadn't driven itself.

The wind shifted, carrying the scent of pine and something else—sweet, like flowers.

Then he heard it.

Woof! Woof!

He knew that bark.

Adrenaline surged through him as he pushed along the old path. Briars snagged at his pants. Honeysuckle and weeds crowded the trail that once lay open. The barking grew louder through the pines. Low branches slapped against his arms, and a rabbit shot from the brush. Overhead, a woodpecker hammered away. Then the trees thinned, and the creek came into view. Sunlight dappled through the branches, turning everything different hues of gold and green. The air was cooler here and carried the smell of mud and moss, like it always had.

It's him.

Chip stood in the shallows, nose down, tail going as he sniffed at something in the rocks.

And her.

Amelia sat on the fallen log, her fingers skimming the water's surface. A dragonfly hovered near her knee, darting away when she lifted her hand.

Liam slowed without meaning to. His stomach fluttered the way it used to whenever she crossed his mind as a boy. Closer now, sunlight caught in her hair, and the breeze pushed a strand across her cheek. Then she looked up.

When their eyes met across ten feet of creek bank, the world stilled. Time had painted her into the kind of pretty that made him want to memorize every detail. Sure, he'd noticed her last night on the docks. But in the sun, everything was clearer.

Her auburn hair was shorter now, curled softly around her face, which made her look older and somehow even more herself. The red on her lips wasn't as sharp as it had seemed under the dock lights; in the sun it looked warmer, almost gentle. A glint of light drew his eyes to her earrings, and then to the pearls at her neck. And that dress—simple, off-white, glowing in the sun—so different from the muddy dresses he remembered when they'd come back from the fields together. It made her seem like she belonged both to this place and beyond it.

Even so, underneath it all, she was still the girl who'd helped him gather pecans when his world was falling apart. The girl who'd made up a song about their dog and taught him that music could happen anywhere. The girl who'd kissed him under the pecan tree when forever seemed possible.

Liam didn't breathe again until Chip spotted him. The dog bounded out of the creek and crashed into his knees with a force that was pure joy.

"Hey, boy." Liam dropped down as Chip's tail lashed water everywhere. "What're you doing out here?"

He was talking to the dog, but his eyes were still on Amelia. She stood from the log and stepped onto the flat stones they'd set there when they were kids. Barefoot, she moved across, her skirt lifted just enough to keep it from trailing in the water.

Stone by stone she came toward him, each step blurring her into the girl he remembered ...

The creek gurgled at Liam's feet as he stood on the bank. From the other side, Amelia wobbled on the first stone, and her braid slipped forward over her shoulder. "Don't let me fall, Liam!" Her voice carried across the water.

He leaned forward, arms out as if he could catch her. "I won't," he shouted.

She stretched for the next stone, arms flapping like a bird. For a second, he thought she'd go in, and his heart jumped clear up his throat. But she caught her balance and squealed when the water splashed around her ankles.

"That don't count," she smiled, shooting him a look.

One stone. Then another. With each step, her voice grew lighter, more certain, until she leaped off the final rock and landed in the dirt beside him. She threw her arms out wide, tipped her head back and laughed—a sound so bright it filled the whole clearing. "I did it! I did it!"

"Told ya you could," he said, grinning till his cheeks hurt.

Amelia flung her arms around him in a quick hug. Her cheek felt warm against his shoulder. "You're my best friend."

"You're mine too."

~elle~

Liam blinked hard, and the girl in his arms vanished. In her place, the woman stepped off the last rock and onto the dirt. They faced each other while Chip circled them both, tail whipping at their legs.

"Liam."

"Amelia." Her name felt like a word from another life.

"Good to see you."

"Good to see you too." She folded her hands in front of her.

That's when he saw it.

A ring.

A diamond, big as a shirt button, set in gold on her left hand.

The sight knocked the breath right out of him.

How'd he not notice it last night? Of course, she was engaged. Of course, she'd found someone who could give her what she deserved.

Amelia followed his gaze down to her hand. Her lips parted, then pressed together, and something flickered across her face—understanding? Regret? Maybe she wished she could take the sting out of his realization. But she remained silent.

Chip bumped his leg, and Liam reached down, scratching the dog's head just to buy himself a moment. To think. To figure out what you were supposed to say to someone who'd once been the center of your world and now stood right there wearing another man's promise.

The moment stayed quiet between them. Water slipped over the rocks in a steady rush, a bird called from the trees, and Chip's panting seemed to fill the whole space.

Standing there, watching her, he finally understood something he'd been too young to grasp all those years ago—there's a part of your heart you only give away once, and sometimes it's the part that teaches you what goodbye really means.

The diamond flashed again, and something inside him

split clean in two. It was all the proof he needed that someone else had claimed the future he'd never stopped imag-
ining, even when he'd told himself he had.

All of it—gone.

15

"What're you doing here?"

The question sounded harsher than he had intended. Seeing her here—at his creek, *their* creek—unsettled him more than he cared to admit.

Amelia's cheeks flushed pink. She glanced down, then raised her eyes again. "Came in for a party. My parents' thing." She tucked a strand of hair behind her ear. "And I wanted to see you. See how you were doing." Her voice softened. "Sorry I didn't say much at the docks last night. I was just ... It's been a while."

"It has." Liam watched as Chip settled between them. "How long are you here?"

"Until the end of the week." Amelia gestured to where a small paddleboat sat along the bank. "That yours?"

"Yeah. Built it myself." He'd put it together after Ma passed, taking it out whenever he needed to clear his mind. It wasn't much to look at, but it always carried him where he needed to go.

Liam knew things couldn't go back to how they'd been when they were kids—too much had changed. Still, standing here with her felt almost like life offering him a second chance. Ma used to say that life had a way of giving you what you needed, not always what you wanted. Now he understood.

Amelia belonged to someone else now, but he could still be her friend, at least while she was in town. They'd made that promise to each other years ago, and he didn't plan on breaking it now. If he'd learned anything from losing so much, it was this: there was a rare beauty in a moment you only got once. And if you were lucky, you learned to be grateful it ever happened at all. Maybe this was one of those moments, and maybe for once, it'd be enough.

"Wanna take it out?" The words tumbled from his mouth before he could second-guess himself.

Her face lit up with the same grin he'd remembered. "Sure."

They made their way to the inlet, fed by the main creek, where the paddleboat sat on the bank. Liam gripped the bow and gave it a push. The hull scraped against the mud as it slid toward the water. At the edge, Chip whined, pacing back and forth.

"Come here, boy." Amelia patted her leg. When he ambled over, she scooped him up and carefully placed him in the back of the boat. "There you go."

Chip sat behind the rear seat, tail thumping against the wooden bottom.

"Careful." Liam steadied the boat as Amelia stepped in, her hand resting on his shoulder.

Twelve years since she'd touched him, and it all rushed back—summer afternoons, her hand in his, pulling him toward some new adventure. He'd forgotten how right it felt.

Focus, Liam.

He gave the boat another push until it floated free, then hopped in. The whole thing rocked, water sloshing everywhere, as he lowered himself.

Amelia grabbed the sides, laughing. "Remember the boat we built that summer?"

"Not sure I'd call it a boat." Liam smirked, reaching for the paddle. "But it was something."

"You did a good job on this one. Didn't even need me this time." She smiled, looking around. "What happened to ours? The one we built?"

"Kept it till"—Liam dipped the paddle—"the hurricane three years ago. Took near everything."

Her smile faded. "I heard. Broke my heart, what happened here." She looked out at the water. "We talked about coming back to the old farm. Even with the insurance money, Daddy wouldn't rebuild. Said the land was worth more than the cost, so he sold it."

Liam nodded as a great blue heron waded in the shallows.

She drew a breath, as if starting fresh. "And your mom? How's she been?"

He kept his eyes fixed on the water. "Hurricane took her too."

Amelia's hand quickly found his. "I'm so sorry, Liam. I shouldn't have—"

He squeezed her hand. "It's all right."

When her fingers tightened around his, he was eight again ...

They sat by the creek, both dangling their feet in the cool water. Chip splashed nearby, chasing minnows that darted away from his paws. Amelia had been crying; her piano teacher had scolded her that morning.

She wiped her nose on her sleeve. "I hate playing piano."

"You don't hate it. You're good at it."

"No, I'm not. Mrs. Whitmore says I'll never be a proper lady if I can't play right."

Liam looked at her teary face and did the only thing he could think of. He reached over and took her hand. "Play something for me. Right here."

"But there's no piano."

"Pretend. Use my hand."

So she did. Her small fingers pressed against his palm, moving as if she were playing keys. She hummed a melody he'd never heard before—something soft, sad, but still beautiful. Chip trotted over and shook water on them, making Amelia giggle through her tears.

"That's the prettiest song I've ever heard," Liam said.

She smiled then, really smiled, and kept hold of his hand as they sat listening to the water flow over the rocks.

Amelia moved her hand away, and the memory dissolved.

Liam blinked. "So, what've you been doing with yourself?"

"Well, mostly college and teaching piano now." She shifted, and the boat rocked gently. "Daddy's been busy with business up there, and Mom's been the same as always—hosting all their friends, throwing parties."

"Up where?"

"Atlanta. But we spend summers at our place in Martha's Vineyard now."

Liam had seen pictures of Martha's Vineyard in a magazine at Miller's. Nothing but sailboats and big houses by the water. It was the sort of place where people like the Jensens belonged, and people like him never would.

"Sounds nice." He tried to keep his voice even. "You like teaching?"

"I do. Funny, I used to hate lessons when I was little. Daddy always said I'd thank him one day. And I suppose he was right—at least, that's what I tell myself." Her eyes got brighter. "The kids remind me why I fell in love with music. There's this one little girl, maybe six, and she plays with such heart. Makes me think of ..." She paused.

"What?"

"Of us."

Us?

Her eyes flicked away, but not for long. "I mean the song we made up about Chip when we found him."

Liam could almost hear their younger voices echoing alongside Chip's bark in between verses. He smiled. "Chip the pup with the spot on his nose ..."

Amelia laughed, shaking her head. "You still remember."

"How could I forget?"

Her fingers tapped the seat lightly. "Found him by the creek where the water flows."

The boat seemed to drift slower. Ripples spread across the water where a fish surfaced, then vanished again. Liam picked up where she left off. "Chip the pup, he's brave and true."

"Chip the pup, we'll take care of you," she finished, neither of them looking away.

"Looks like I'm not the only one who remembers."

"We must've sung it a thousand times that summer."

"Maybe a thousand and one."

She chuckled, then fell quiet. "I miss that."

"Me too."

They drifted deeper into the inlet, where the trees bunched together and Spanish moss trailed from the branches. Liam pointed to their left. "You could see the old pecan tree from here. Used to anyway."

Amelia followed his gaze, then turned back with wide eyes. "That's gone too?"

Liam nodded, feeling a familiar ache. "Yeah."

She stared at the empty space where the tree had stood. Her fingers brushed over her wrist, as if reaching for something that wasn't there. For a second, a smile crossed her face.

Liam wondered if she was thinking about that summer too—the way he always did when he passed this spot. The tree where they'd met. Where he'd carved their initials. Where they'd—

Then sunlight caught her ring again.

He'd told himself not to look, but he did. Knowing was

one thing; seeing was another. Part of him wanted to ask who the man was—the one who could give her everything Liam never could. Did he own a big house? What kind of work did he do? Did he make her laugh the way she used to laugh here by the creek? He stopped himself there. Even if he asked, even if she told him everything, what good would it do?

There was a particular kind of heartbreak that came not from losing her, but from realizing that maybe she was never really his to begin with. Somewhere deep inside, a piece of him broke off and was gone. He cleared his throat and let the paddle drag, skimming the surface. "We ought to head back."

They sat quietly as he steered them toward shore. Marsh grass swayed in the breeze, carrying salt and damp earth on the air. A kingfisher rattled from the cypress along the bank, and as the boat glided past a half-submerged log, a turtle dropped into the water with barely a splash. Chip lifted his head at the noise, ears perked, then sank back down with a sigh.

When the boat finally scraped against the muddy bottom, Liam jumped out, pulling it onto the bank. Chip padded past him and put his nose to the ground, following some scent.

Amelia took his offered hand as she stepped onto the bank. Her fingers lingered longer than necessary. One of them should have let go. Instead, they held on, neither willing to be the first to do so.

Liam glanced toward the path ahead, then back again. "Come on. I wanna show you something."

16

AT THE HOUSE, LIAM pushed the door open and stepped aside. Amelia paused in the doorway, then crossed the threshold. Her eyes swept over the space before turning to him. "You did all this?"

"Yeah. Had a lot of help though. Not done yet, but it's close."

Chip barreled in from outside, skidding across the floor before regaining his footing. He began sniffing every corner, his tail wagging nonstop. In the living room, Liam's stomach knotted when her eyes landed on the mantel above the brick fireplace.

Wait, not that.

Maybe he shouldn't show her? Some things were better left in the past, weren't they?

She was already walking toward it when he moved instinctively, sliding into her line of sight. But then he caught the look on her face, the same wonder she'd had the day he'd carved it.

Amelia had been there too. It was *theirs*. Didn't she deserve to see it again?

"Hold on." Liam reached over, lifting the piece of pecan

wood from the mantel. "After the hurricane, I went back and found our old tree down." His voice snagged. "It hurt seeing it like that. But I saved this piece. Just reminds me of the good days we had."

Amelia's gaze locked on the carved heart with their initials inside: *A + L.* She said nothing at first, only stared.

Chip's nails clicked against the wooden floor as he shifted positions. A board creaked somewhere upstairs, and a shutter rattled slightly against the house—probably from the breeze. Or maybe one had come loose.

Finally, Amelia reached out. Her fingertip traced the heart first. Then she glided to the *A.* She lingered there, almost tenderly, before moving across to the *L.* Her hand stilled.

She closed her eyes, and for a breath, he thought she might pull away. Instead, her finger stayed on the *L,* as if holding on to something she wasn't ready to lose. When she spoke, her voice was low. "Those were good days. The best I've ever known."

Twelve years of missing her, of wondering what might have been, pressed against his chest until he could hardly breathe.

She stepped closer. Then again. She lifted her face toward his, and he saw everything he'd lost reflected in her eyes—and everything he still wanted.

Without thinking, he closed the gap between them.

What's happening?

He should've remembered the ring on her finger. He should've thought about the life she'd built without him. What about the promises she'd made to someone else? Or that she'd be gone in a few days and then he'd be right back where he started.

Amelia was now close enough to touch, close enough that he could smell her perfume—something floral that reminded him of the magnolia tree that used to bloom by the old church.

His gaze drifted to her lips. All he could hear was the rush of his own pulse. She didn't move, and neither did he. But when he finally looked up, he found her watching his mouth. For a heartbeat, the entire world seemed to balance on the edge of something that could change everything.

This is wrong.

Every part of him knew it. Yet nothing in his life had ever felt more right.

She swayed toward him—just an inch.

He couldn't look away. One tilt forward would destroy everything. One step back would destroy *him*.

Her breath brushed against his cheek.

If he leaned in, there'd be no going back.

He shouldn't—

Woof! Woof!

They sprang apart as if they'd touched something hot. And somehow there was both too much space between them—and not nearly enough.

"I'm sorry." Liam took another step back. "I wasn't trying to—I just ..."

"It's okay. I'm sorry too."

His eyes followed hers to the diamond ring that seemed to grow larger the longer he stared.

"We've got the lives we've got, Liam," she whispered. "Even if it's not the ones we thought we'd have."

Not what we thought we'd have?

Was that all he'd been to her? Just some childhood dream she'd outgrown?

"I should go." She was already moving for the door.

"Amelia, wait—"

But she was calling for Chip, who abandoned his investigation of a suspicious corner and trotted over. At the front door, she stopped and glanced back. "It's beautiful, Liam. What you've built here."

Then she opened it and left.

Liam watched as Amelia walked to her car. Chip trotted over and jumped into the passenger seat. She slid behind the wheel without looking back. The slam of her door, the rumble of the engine, and the dust that trailed behind were all that was left of her and the summer of '48.

For a wild second, he considered running after her. Instead, he closed the door and leaned his forehead against it. When he turned, the carved wood propped on the mantel grabbed his attention. The heart looked smaller now. But the letters were still there: *A + L*—a promise made by children who'd believed that was enough to hold anything together.

───≈───

Liam's truck started on the second try, then he rolled down the window and pulled out. Static crackled from the radio, but he let it be. Warm air poured in as the town slipped by in a blur of storefronts and porches. At the first stop sign, he sat too long. A horn blared behind him, snapping him out of the loop playing in his head.

He gripped the wheel tighter, then steered right and kept going. The road bent past the church and a stretch of fields before the familiar sprawl of ocean opened up ahead. A gravel drive split off between two leaning posts where a hand-painted sign read *Ashford Boatyard*. A short run of chain-link fence ran on each side, but the gate itself stood open. As Liam turned in, the air carried the sharpness of salt and pine tar, mixed with the metallic bite of hot nails and fresh-cut boards. Liam parked off to the side and climbed out. He drew a breath and walked through the entrance, nodding to the workers. Most were shirtless, some with sweat shining off their backs, others caked with sawdust that clung like a second skin. Some had both.

"What're you doing here on your day off?" Simeon asked.

Liam fell in step. "Figured I'd get ahead for tomorrow."

Jerome's laugh carried over the yard noise. "The man can't even take a day off without thinking about boats."

"He ain't gonna get many days off now that he's crew chief," Simeon said, wiping his brow.

Both men chuckled, but Liam kept walking.

Jerome's grin faltered. "What's eating at you?"

Liam quickened his pace. "Nothing."

Simeon and Jerome headed toward the shade of an old oak tree where they'd left their lunch pails, as always. Several other workers had settled down with sandwiches wrapped in wax paper and mason jars of sweet tea. For a few minutes, the yard quieted.

Simeon took his time, easing down against the tree trunk before reaching into his pail. He held up his sandwich.

"Want half? Got plenty."

"No, thanks." Liam kept his eyes on the office. Through the windows, shadows moved where there shouldn't have been any on a Tuesday afternoon.

Jerome nodded toward the office. "Mr. Ashford's got company. Saw a fancy car in the lot earlier."

Liam sighed and then let himself get lost in the conversation between Simeon and Jerome—something about Simeon's wife wanting to paint their kitchen, and whether yellow or blue would look better with their old cabinets.

Then came footsteps across the yard. Liam looked up.

Two figures approached, silhouetted against the bright sun.

Mr. Ashford?

And someone else beside him.

Liam stood slowly.

The second man stepped out of the glare. Dark hair. White dress shirt.

Liam's vision tunneled. The surrounding conversations faded. The ground narrowed to nothing but the face he'd prayed he'd never see again.

No. No. No. Not him.

"Good you're here, Wright." Mr. Ashford's clapped the young man's shoulder. "Meet your new foreman. You might know my son, Tommy."

17

THE ALARM CLOCK RATTLED at four-thirty, though Liam had already spent an hour staring at the ceiling. He rolled out of bed, pulled on yesterday's work clothes, and grabbed his thermos from the counter.

Mrs. Patterson had brought him dinner over last night—mashed potatoes and biscuits—and sat with him while he'd picked at his food and told her about Tommy becoming foreman. Since she'd left, her words had circled in his mind: *Don't let that boy get to you. You need this job.*

Yeah, he needed it all right. Didn't mean he had to like it.

Twenty minutes later, Liam pulled into the boatyard, where only Simeon's old Ford and Jerome's beat-up Chevy sat in the lot. Tommy had told all of them yesterday to get there an hour early. No explanation why, only that they'd better be there.

He found the other two sitting on the dock, legs hanging over the edge.

Liam settled beside them. "Morning."

"This ain't right," Simeon grumbled without looking up. "Three years here, and not once did we have to come in early for nothing."

Jerome flicked ash from his cigarette into the water. "Didn't even say what for."

They sat in silence, watching the harbor wake. A pelican skimmed so close its wingtips brushed the surface, leaving ripples behind. Farther out, a tug nosed past with its faintly glowing deck light, and a ship's horn rumbled three deep blasts that boomed across the bay.

The sky brightened as mist lifted off the water. Sunlight flashed on the waves, and gulls squawked louder as boats arrived along the docks. Jerome lit another cigarette while Simeon stretched his legs. There was still no sign of Tommy.

Nearly an hour had passed before headlights swept through the lot. The engine cut off, and a door slammed shut. Footsteps clomped along the dock. Then Tommy stepped into the light from the dock lamps, checking his watch as if *they* were the ones keeping him waiting.

"Gentlemen," Tommy said as he reached them. "Traffic was a nightmare. Let's get to work, shall we? Plenty to do today."

Nobody answered. Jerome took another puff.

"I want this place cleaned up. Need to make sure things are running the way they should."

"What's that supposed to mean?" Simeon asked.

"You'll see. Now get moving."

Liam caught Simeon's eye, then Jerome's. "I thought we were starting the Jensen yacht? Mr. Ashford told me—"

"I'll tell you when to start on that." Tommy's eyes found his. "Right now, you focus on what I'm saying."

The morning crawled by with Tommy barking orders to re-stack boards already in neat rows, wipe already clean tools, and sweep the same spots they'd swept yesterday. Every fifteen minutes he appeared with his clipboard, inventing another pointless task just to keep them moving. Then, for a while, he left them alone.

Around ten, he was back again, standing over Liam as he restacked boards from earlier.

"You know," Tommy said, loud enough for all of them to hear, "in a few months when Dad retires, I'll be running this whole place." He adjusted his collar. "'Course, I'd rather be closing deals with actual clients right now. But apparently, I've got to babysit you people first."

You people?

Jerome and Simeon exchanged a look.

"Must be rough," Liam said, keeping his eyes fixed on the boards.

Tommy glanced at his watch again, then scribbled something on his clipboard. "Move those planks to the other side when you're done. And make sure they're straight this time."

They already are.

Simeon's mouth twitched toward a smile, then he went back to sanding. Jerome bent to gather a length of rope, looping it into neat coils at his feet. Liam straightened slowly, watching Tommy saunter off.

———

Around noon, Tommy called them all over to where a fuel

tank sat by the back fence. "I need someone to clean this out. We got money here just wasting away."

Liam looked at the rusty tank with welds that had been patched multiple times over the years. He could smell the varnish of old gas from where he stood. "That's not safe. Could still be fumes in there."

"It's just a tank."

"I've done it before," Liam said. "Line burst on a skiff once and we had to drain it fast. But that was an emergency. You don't just mess with it without the right gear."

Tommy stepped closer and looked up. "You refusing orders?"

Liam had to fight the urge to smile—the days when Tommy towered over him were long gone. On top of that, years of hard labor had thickened Liam's shoulders and arms, while Tommy looked like he'd never done a push-up in his life.

The yard went quiet. Jerome and Simeon stopped pretending to work.

"I'm saying it's dangerous," Liam said. "Needs to be done right."

"Still a coward, huh?" Tommy's voice was soft, almost friendly. "Just like your old man."

Coward?

Liam's fists curled. In a blink, he was eight again, lying in the dirt while Tommy and his gang called him a coward's son and walked away laughing. He thought of what Ma had told him afterward—how Pa had held him before shipping out. Liam had been too young to remember any of it, but Ma said Pa had cried that last morning. Pa had left everything behind to fight a war that killed him. Tommy wouldn't last two minutes in a fight, let alone a war.

"You deaf, Wright?"

The same childhood rage he'd felt at Amelia's birthday party surged through him. He wanted to knock that smug look off Tommy's face again. But not here. Not in front of everyone. Getting fired wouldn't prove anything.

"I'll clean it," Liam said at last. "But not barehanded."

If it had to be done, better him than letting Tommy shove one of the others at it blind.

Without a word, Liam crossed to the shed and gathered what he could find: oil-stained gloves, a hose, and a siphon pump. Just outside sat a barrel of water used for rinsing tools; he dipped a rag into it and tied it over his mouth and nose. It wasn't much, but it was the best he could do.

Tommy smirked. "However you want, Wright. Just get it done."

The men hung back, watching as Liam crouched by the tank, listening to the slosh inside when he tapped it with his knuckles. The sound was too heavy to be near empty.

Fifty gallons; maybe more?

One spark and the whole yard could blow.

Liam set his jaw and squeezed the pump, coaxing the fuel through the hose in uneven gulps. The fumes hit instantly, stinging his eyes, and filling his throat with the sour taste of rust and gasoline. He bit back a cough, pressing the wet rag tighter against his face.

Minutes blurred as the pump wheezed and squeaked, over and over. Every muscle in his arms strained, and though his lungs screamed for clean air, he kept going.

Somewhere in the haze, Ma's voice came back to him: *You're stronger than you think.*

By the time Jerome lit another cigarette, the barrel was nearly full.

Finally, the sound changed—a hollow gurgle, then nothing but air. Liam pulled the hose free, capped the barrel, then yanked the rag off his face and doubled over, sucking in the salty air until it soothed the burn in his chest.

Done.

Jerome let out a low whistle. Simeon just shook his head.

Tommy barely looked up from his clipboard. "About time," he said, like Liam had just finished sweeping a floor.

———

At lunch, Liam, Jerome, and Simeon headed to their usual spot under the oak tree. They'd barely unwrapped their sandwiches when Tommy stomped over. "Break's over. Back on those boards."

Jerome threw his hands in the air. "We just sat down."

"Company time, company rules."

They packed up their food and got back to work. Before long, Liam caught sight of him through the office window—Tommy in Mr. Ashford's chair, feet up, sandwich in one hand, phone in the other, laughing at something.

"Funny how that works." Simeon leaned on his mallet. "Some folks get born into it."

"Others gotta earn it," Jerome said.

Liam shrugged. "Or try to."

By five, exhaustion had well and truly set in. Liam's back ached and his hands throbbed, though they hadn't accomplished anything all day. He turned, reaching for his toolbox, grateful the shift was finally over. Planks creaked close behind him. He straightened and glanced over his shoulder. Mr. Ashford was heading their way.

This can't be good.

"Wright. How's the new build coming along?"

Liam froze. His mouth went dry as he shifted his weight, trying to buy a second he didn't have. What could he say? First day as crew chief and he'd got nothing done? Should he blame Tommy? Every answer felt wrong. Finally, he forced something out. "We haven't started yet, sir. Had to do other things."

"Other things?" His eyes found Tommy. "What other things?"

"Getting organized," Tommy said. "Making sure everything was—"

"Organized?" Mr. Ashford stepped toward his son. "You had a forty-footer to start today. The Jensens expect progress reports, and you spent the day organizing?"

Tommy's face went red. "I was trying to—"

"You were playing boss instead of doing your job." Mr. Ashford's voice carried across the yard. Every worker within earshot stopped to listen. "We're already behind schedule on our other contracts, and now we're further behind because you wasted a day doing nonsense!"

For a moment, Liam caught a glimpse of the boy behind the bully. Watching Mr. Ashford tear into Tommy in front of everyone almost had him feeling sorry for the guy. Almost.

"The Jensens don't care about organization," Mr. Ashford continued. "They care about getting their yacht finished on time. You understand?"

"Yes, sir."

Mr. Ashford turned back to Liam. "I need you here tonight. The Jensens are having a party on one of our showcase yachts. I want you to see what they expect from this build. First though, I need you to help set up. Tables, chairs, and whatever the caterers need."

Liam nodded, even though he wanted nothing more than to go home and climb into bed. But at least he'd maybe get to see Amelia, and maybe she'd want to see him too.

"About an hour," Mr. Ashford said. "Then I need you there."

"Yes sir. I'll be there."

As Mr. Ashford walked away, Tommy glared at Liam like it was his fault.

At his truck, Liam kept his head down as Tommy walked past, focusing on putting his tools away. He was latching his toolbox when the crunch of gravel grabbed his attention. A black Lincoln pulled into the lot. His heart leaped.

Amelia?

Maybe she'd come looking for him, to talk about yesterday. He straightened, suddenly aware of his dirty clothes and how bad he probably smelled.

Where's Tommy going?

Liam stopped moving.

Tommy wasn't just leaving for the day—he was heading straight for the Lincoln.

When the door opened, Amelia stepped out in a pink dress, the same shade she'd worn to her birthday party. Sunlight brushed her hair with a hint of gold, and for a moment she looked just like she had back then. Amelia said something to Tommy, tilting her head as she spoke. He bent toward her and grabbed her elbow, pulling her just enough that she lost her balance into him.

Then his hand slid to her shoulder.

The other to her hip.

Before Liam could take another breath, Tommy leaned down and pressed his lips against hers.

What?!

Heat rushed to Liam's head. His vision blurred, and he swayed where he stood. He'd never known what dying felt like, but he was sure it couldn't be far from this.

Amelia didn't pull away right off, but when she did, there was something on her face that didn't seem right. She looked across the lot, and their eyes met for a second, long enough for Liam to catch something that felt like an apology, as if she hated that he had seen them.

The girl he'd loved since he was eight was going to marry the boy who'd made his life miserable—and still was, twelve years later.

18

"Over here," one of the caterers called.

Liam lugged another folding table up the gangplank as the yacht bobbed on the water. The picture of Tommy kissing Amelia wouldn't leave his mind, even as he set the table where the caterer had pointed. He stepped back while she draped it with white cloth, then topped it with crystal glasses, silver forks, and flowers.

Savory aromas drifted up from somewhere below—buttery sauces and something spiced in a way that reminded him he'd never eaten food like this.

"Don't just stand there." She glared at him. "Grab some rope for these panels—it should be in the wheelhouse."

Liam nodded and made his way toward the front of the yacht, stepping carefully around the supplies. When he reached the wheelhouse, the door was cracked. He could hear voices—one he recognized. He pushed the door open just enough to peer inside.

Tommy had a young blonde server pressed against the chart table, with his hand braced beside her head.

What the—

And then he kissed her.

The woman pulled back. "What about your fiancée? Where is she?"

"Don't worry about it," Tommy said. "We got a while."

Liam's pulse kicked up as he eased away from the door and hurried back to the main deck. When he arrived, the caterer glanced up expectantly. "Well?"

"Nothing," Liam said.

She frowned. "We'll make do."

Liam lingered for another moment while she adjusted a panel, then slipped back toward the tables, keeping himself busy. From there he could keep out of sight, though still close enough in case Mr. Ashford needed him.

Voices rose from the dock as guests began arriving. Couples streamed aboard—men in pressed slacks and polos and women in dresses that lifted and snapped in the harbor breeze. Amelia appeared in the same pink dress as earlier and moved through the tangle of partygoers. When their eyes met across the deck, she started toward him—until Tommy grabbed her and steered her toward another group.

Liam dropped his gaze and busied himself with the nearest table. He smoothed the cloth, lined up the forks, then pressed one so hard it nearly bent beneath his thumb.

Breathe.

———

A low rumble shook the deck as the yacht pulled away. The sudden shift sent him grabbing the table for balance until the motion evened out. Only after they were gliding into open water did he release his grip.

"Wright." Mr. Ashford appeared beside him. "Come on. Time to show you around."

Liam fell in step with him as they crossed the deck toward the stern. Mr. Ashford ran his hand along the rail. "See this mahogany? The Jensens get me wholesale prices on wood like this from their Atlanta suppliers."

"They're in lumber?"

"Among other things. We've worked together nearly thirteen years—since before they moved to Atlanta. They supply the wood; we build the boats." Mr. Ashford smiled. "And tonight's about our new partnerships. We just landed three more suppliers thanks to their connections."

That's why they left Hadley Cove.

"Well, congratulations, sir. I guess that means we'll have steady work for a long time."

Mr. Ashford chuckled. "You know, Wright, I like how curious you are about the business side. That's part of why I made you crew chief." He gestured toward the guests. "Sometimes it's not about how good you are—it's about who you know. The Jensens opened doors for this boatyard that nobody else ever could."

Liam nodded as Mr. Ashford moved toward the cabin. "The galley's got custom cabinetry, all dovetail joints, and—"

A man's voice cut in. "Well, if it isn't our boat builder."

They turned to find Mr. and Mrs. Jensen standing only a few feet away, champagne glasses in hand.

"Mr. and Mrs. Jensen," Mr. Ashford said. "I was just showing Wright some details you requested."

"Wright?" Mr. Jensen squinted over his champagne.

"Muscadine Drive—you're the boy who used to play with our Amelia."

Mrs. Jensen's hand flew to her chest. "My goodness, yes! Remind me of your name again?"

"Liam."

"That's right—Liam." Her eyes flicked over his shirt and boots before she gave a quick nod. "Didn't expect to see you … dressed for work."

Heat crept up his neck. "I didn't have time to change after—"

"Well, you're here now." Mr. Jensen's smile thinned. "I suppose you can stay."

Liam swallowed. "I'm sorry. I don't want to ruin your party. I just—"

"Nonsense." Mrs. Jensen waved him off. "We're just glad you finally made something of yourself. We always hoped you would." She laughed lightly, turning her glass in her hand.

Liam kept his eyes down.

A backhanded compliment is probably the only type I'll get from this family.

"Wright's one of our best craftsmen." Mr. Ashford's voice carried over the chatter. "You won't be disappointed."

Mr. Jensen gave a polite nod. "Very well then." The couple smiled before blending back into the circle of conversation among the other guests.

Around him, glasses clinked and laughter rose. Champagne, cocktails, highballs—glass after glass, but hardly a plate in sight. A server passed with a steaming silver tray of bite-sized pastries. The scent of rosemary and garlic trailed her. Heads turned and noses lifted. But then everyone went right back to their drinks.

Nobody took one?

Liam shook his head. Ma would've had something to say about wasting food like that. All this fancy cooking going untouched while people got drunk instead.

Movement near the bar caught Liam's attention. Tommy slouched at the counter, laughing too loudly and clapping a man on the back. His face was flushed, eyes glassy, and the drink in his hand was sloshing dangerously near the rim.

Each time the blonde server passed, Tommy's gaze followed. Once, she paused long enough to let her fingers brush his as she handed off a tray. Tommy grinned, and when she walked by again, she caught his hand outright before disappearing into the crowd.

Across the deck, Amelia laughed at something an older woman said.

I gotta tell her.

But how? Pull her aside?

That'll look too suspicious.

Wait until Tommy sobers up?

Not tonight.

Tell her right now, in front of everyone?

Liam sighed and rubbed the back of his neck. No matter how he tried to frame it, it would come out like he was just trying to cause trouble.

Somewhere behind him, a voice called out. "Looks like a

storm's moving in."

He turned as heads tipped toward the horizon where dark clouds had thickened. The wind picked up, ruffling dresses and making men reach for their hats.

The yacht angled back toward the harbor as the first drops fell. Guests huddled under the covered areas of the deck. Liam wiped the rain from his brow, scanning the crowd until he found Amelia near the starboard railing, where the awning covered only part of the deck.

Now or never.

His stomach churned. His legs felt heavy.

What if she didn't believe him?

He slowed, almost stopping. For a breath, he thought about turning back.

No—

He kept moving. She deserved the truth, no matter what telling it might cost him.

Rain fell steadier now as he closed the distance. Amelia turned as he approached.

"Amelia, I need to—"

A hand clamped down on his shoulder and spun him around. Tommy stood there, swaying. His breath reeked.

Whiskey.

"Whatever you got to say to my fiancée, you can say to me. To all of us."

Liam glanced around. Several people had stopped talking and stared. "You don't want that, Tommy."

"Oh, I do." Tommy's grip tightened. "You've got something to say to my woman? Say it to me."

"Tommy, please—" Amelia started.

Tommy shoved Liam, sending him back a half-step. "No—let him talk."

Liam looked past him to Amelia, whose face had gone pale. A loose circle had formed around them. Rain drummed even harder against the deck. "I saw you in the wheelhouse, kissing her." He pointed at the blonde server. "That one over there."

Every eye swiveled between Liam, Tommy, and the server.

Amelia's hand went to her throat. "Tommy, is it true?"

"No—" Then Tommy stumbled toward Liam. "You ... liar. I was—uh, we were—helping, I—" His hand twitched, and the whiskey tumbler slipped from his grasp.

CRASH!

Murmurs rippled through the circle as shoes shifted back from the shards.

"Ask her," Liam said, nodding toward the server. "Right now."

The blonde woman's face crumpled. That answer was enough for anyone paying attention.

Tommy's eyes shot to Liam. "You piece of—"

He lunged, fist flying.

Liam sidestepped.

Tommy missed.

The wild swing sent him stumbling forward across the slick deck.

Gasps erupted from the circle.

Tommy staggered, arms flailing, hands clawing at nothing.

The rail.

A scream tore through the air.
Then Tommy toppled over the side.

19

"Somebody grab a life ring!" Mr. Ashford shouted.

Guests rushed to the railing, leaning over as they peered into the dark water below.

"Please!" Amelia's cry carried above it all. "Somebody, please—help him!"

The rain came down harder, needling Liam's skin. Crew members scrambled for life preservers. Shouts blurred into one deafening roar. And then, through the chaos, Ma's voice came to him: *You're stronger than you think.*

He gripped the rail, adrenaline surging. If he waited any longer, Tommy would be gone. There was no time left to think. Liam kicked off his boots.

"What are you doing?" someone yelled.

He ignored them, swung himself up over the railing, and jumped.

The water hit like ice, tearing the breath from his lungs. Salt stung his eyes as he surfaced.

"Over there!" someone screamed.

Muffled shouts rained down from the deck—pointing, calling—but every wave looked the same. Then, a flash of white.

There.

Twenty feet away.

Liam swam hard, fighting the yacht's wake and his heavy clothes. Tommy had gone under by the time he reached the spot. Liam took a deep breath and dove.

The water was murky, but he could make out a pale shape sinking below. He kicked deeper, lungs burning, and grabbed Tommy's shirt. The fabric tore, but he got an arm around his chest and kicked toward the surface.

They broke through together, both gasping. Tommy was barely conscious, coughing up seawater and clinging to Liam.

"I got you," Liam said.

Hauling Tommy's dead weight drained the last of Liam's strength, but he kept kicking, dragging them toward the rope ladder swaying against the hull.

Several hands pulled Tommy up first, then they helped Liam climb the ladder.

Water streamed from Tommy's clothes as he collapsed on the deck. Someone spread a blanket over him; another pressed a towel into his hands. Still, he didn't move—just lay there, staring up at Liam with a trace of something that almost looked like gratitude.

"Tommy!" Amelia dropped beside him. "Are you hurt? Are you all right?"

He nodded weakly, and sat up, still catching his breath. The crowd gathered around.

Amelia stood slowly and turned to Liam. "Is it true? What you said—about him and that girl?"

For a long moment, Liam said nothing.

Tommy was alive and safe. Maybe it would be better to let it go, pretend none of this had happened.

But then he looked at Amelia—really looked. He saw the hope in her eyes that he might say no, that it had all been a misunderstanding. He knew the truth might break her heart, but a lie would break it worse.

"Yeah," he whispered, lowering his head. "It's true."

The words seemed to fall heavier than the rain.

Amelia's eyes lingered on Liam before shifting to Tommy. "Is it true?"

"Yes—but it didn't mean anything, I—"

"Don't." Amelia's hand went to the ring on her finger. She twisted it off and gazed at it as if she were seeing it for the first time.

Then she threw it at Tommy.

The ring bounced off his chest and skittered across the wet deck to the railing, where it stopped and glimmered under the yacht's lights. "It's over," she said. "We're done!"

Tommy pushed himself up on his elbows. "Amelia, wait. Let me explain—"

"Explain what? That you've been cheating on me?" Her voice trembled, but her eyes stayed steady. "Tell me this—was this the first time? Or just the first time you've been caught?"

"I—I didn't ... It wasn't like that, I—"

"Got it," she said, cutting him off. "That says it all."

Tommy's mouth opened, then closed.

She shook her head and turned to her dad, who'd been standing nearby. "I'm sorry, Daddy. I can't do it. I can't marry him."

Mr. Jensen's face was stoic. Then he simply nodded. "If that's what you want, sweetheart."

—ele—

As the yacht pulled back into harbor, the crowd dispersed. Two guests Liam didn't recognize helped Tommy to his feet while the blonde server awkwardly supported his other side. Mr. Ashford followed close behind, scolding his son as the group disappeared below deck.

Watching Tommy get what he deserved should've felt good, like justice was being served. But it didn't. Liam exhaled and walked away, soon finding himself alone at the stern. The wake stretched out behind, fading into the dark. The rain had softened to a mist, and clouds split apart above the harbor. Moonlight spilled in pale streaks across the water. In the gaps, a few stars shimmered faintly.

"Liam?"

He turned. Amelia stood a few feet away, her hair coming loose from its pins. But she looked more beautiful than ever.

"I can't believe you saved him." She stepped forward. "After everything he's done to you."

"It was the right thing to do."

"You could've drowned."

"Maybe. But I didn't."

"Don't you ever do that again." She gave a teary laugh, wiping at her eyes.

"I'll try not to." He smiled and looked out at the water, then back at her. "Yesterday, I wanted to tell you something."

"Why didn't you?"

"Well, because I know you got your life up in Atlanta." He paused, then took her hand. "But I had to tell you, just once. Even if—"

"What?"

"Twelve years, Amelia. Not a single day's gone by I haven't thought of you. I love you. I always have."

She didn't speak. She just stared for what felt like forever. *I shouldn't have said—*

Then a tear slipped down her cheek, and she squeezed his hand. "I love you too. All these years, I kept thinking about that summer. About us. About what we were."

"But Tommy—"

"Was what my parents wanted. What they thought was best for me. He was never you, Liam. Never could be. No one could ever replace you."

Liam's hand lifted almost without thought, his fingers brushing her cheek. She closed her eyes at the touch, leaning into his palm. When she opened them again, he saw in her gaze everything he'd missed. Slowly, she rose onto her toes, closing the space between them.

He angled his face down, and when his lips found hers, the rest of the world faded. The kiss was unhurried at first, tentative, as if they were both relearning something they'd once known by heart. Then the kiss deepened—slow, tender, certain—the kind that said what words never could.

Somewhere behind them, a smattering of applause rose.

They broke apart, breathless, and turned to see several of the yacht's crew gathered in the cabin doorway, watching with smiles.

Liam lowered his head, but Amelia gave a soft laugh that drew his eyes back to hers.

"What happens now?" she asked, clutching at his soaked shirt.

Liam pulled her closer. "I don't know. But we'll figure it out together."

20

One Year Later

THE OLD PECAN TREE had been long gone, leaving only a stump left behind. Still, this place was theirs.

Beside it, Liam stood at the makeshift altar and watched Amelia walk across the same field where they'd first met. The stump sat to his left and where the tree had once spread its branches, rows of white chairs held most of Hadley Cove.

The sun dipped lower, pouring amber light across the field. Honeysuckle carried in on the breeze, and in the tall grass at the edge of the chairs, the first lightning bugs began to glow.

In the front, Mrs. Patterson dabbed at her eyes, while Mr. Miller sat beside her, tugging at his collar. Jerome sat by him with his shoulders back, keeping a careful eye on Chip in the next seat. Behind them, the guys from the boatyard had taken up three entire rows, most already loosening their ties.

Even Mr. and Mrs. Jensen were there, sitting straighter

than anyone, yet smiling for real this time. They'd come around after that evening on the water, when they saw the yacht Liam had built, finally admitting how wrong they'd been about him.

The biggest change of all stood at Liam's side: Simeon, dressed in a plain black robe with the Bible resting in his hands. Not long after the Jensen yacht was finished, Simeon stunned everyone by retiring from the yard and becoming ordained.

"Always meant to," he'd told Liam. And now he was here, ready to marry the boy he'd helped raise.

When Amelia reached the front, Liam stood a little taller. She wasn't just walking toward him—she was walking him into the rest of his life.

She wore a white cotton dress with tiny buttons down the back, her hair falling in loose waves around her shoulders, with a bundle of wildflowers in her hands.

Gorgeous.

Mr. Jensen walked her down the aisle. At the altar, he placed Amelia's hand in Liam's. His grip lingered as he leaned in close. "She's yours now. You take good care of my girl."

"Yes, sir."

Simeon opened his Bible and smiled at them both. "Dear friends, we're gathered here today ..."

The ceremony was simple, and though Mr. Jensen had offered to pay for something more elaborate, they'd chosen this instead. And even though Ma couldn't be there, Liam knew she was looking down on them with the brightest smile.

When Simeon asked for the rings, Jerome stood and patted his leg. "Come on, Chip. This is it." The dog hopped off the chair and pattered up the altar. A small satin pillow tied to his back with white ribbon bounced gently with each step. Jerome kept one hand near Chip's collar while he carefully untied the rings from the pillow. Both ring bearers had done their job perfectly.

"Do you, Liam, take Amelia to be your wife? To love and cherish, in good times and bad, for as long as you both shall live?"

"I do."

"And do you, Amelia, take Liam to be your husband? To love and cherish, in good times and bad, for as long as you both shall live?"

"I do."

They slipped the gold bands onto each other's fingers. Amelia's hand trembled slightly, and Liam steadied it with his own. He felt the warmth of her skin, the weight of the ring, and let the moment settle deep inside him. Nothing had ever felt more right.

"By the power vested in me by the state of Georgia, I now pronounce you husband and wife." Simeon's voice boomed across the field. "Liam, you may kiss your bride."

Liam cupped Amelia's face, and when he kissed her, there was no sound other than the wind through the grass, no movement but the gentle sway of her dress. Just the two of them, here and now. Just as it was always supposed to be.

The crowd erupted in cheers. When they finally broke apart, tears sparkled on her cheeks in the last light of the day. "I can't believe we're really married."

"Believe it."

When they turned to face their friends and family, Mrs. Patterson was sobbing openly. The boatyard crew whistled and hollered. Mr. Miller was clapping, though he still looked uncomfortable in his suit. And Mr. Ashford was there, cheering louder than anyone.

But Tommy wasn't there.

Mr. Ashford had explained that his son was "finding his own way" up north—a decision that had come after the yacht incident and left everyone understanding that some people belonged in Hadley Cove, and others simply didn't. After Tommy left, Mr. Ashford began hinting at a promotion. Everyone at the yard knew who really kept things running, and soon Liam would be the new foreman.

Still, none of that mattered as much as right now. Nothing compared to standing here with Amelia—surrounded by family and friends—on the very ground where an eight-year-old boy had once carved a promise into a tree.

As they started down the makeshift aisle between the cheering crowd, rice flew from all directions. Chip trotted alongside the newlyweds, and Amelia laughed, ducking her head against Liam's shoulder as the grains scattered like confetti around their feet. She leaned in and whispered. "You know what I'm thinking of?"

"What?"

"That day we met, right here."

"And now look at us." Liam smiled. "I love you, Amelia Wright."

Hearing her new name sent a thrill through him.

She squeezed his hand. "I love you, Liam Wright."

At the end of the aisle, Liam's truck waited with tin cans tied to the bumper and white ribbons trailing. On the back window, someone had scrawled *Just Married* in soap.

But before climbing in, Liam turned back to the stump where their tree had stood. Somehow, losing the tree had made the spot more sacred, not less. His hand tightened around Amelia's.

Some promises, he realized, were worth keeping. No matter how long it took to fulfill them.

21

Present Day

"... AND THAT'S HOW I ended up the luckiest man alive."

Charlotte wiped her wet cheek. "That's the most beautiful story I've ever heard."

Liam let out a rough laugh and brushed at the corner of his eye, as if even he was surprised by the tear.

Kara dabbed at hers with a tissue. "Didn't know you'd lived through all that."

Emma sat beside them, tears slipping down as she looked at her grandfather like she was seeing him for the first time.

The volunteer holding Snowball sniffled. "Your ma sounds wonderful."

"She was. Best person I ever knew."

Charlotte shifted Whiskers in her lap. "Where's Amelia now? And Chip?"

Kara shot her daughter a warning look. "Charlotte."

"No, it's all right," Liam said, lifting a hand. "It's a fair question. You see, the thing about love is, sometimes it lasts fifty years, sometimes five minutes. But every moment matters." He met Charlotte's eyes. "The important thing is to love while you can. Don't wait for perfect. Love the people in front of you, while you've got the chance."

The room stayed quiet for a beat.

Riley whimpered from his crate in the corner, and Liam glanced over. "And speaking of love, how's our boy over there doing?"

"Still scared," the volunteer said. "But he listened to the whole story. I think he likes your voice."

Liam smiled. "That's something."

As people gathered their things, Emma wandered over to Riley's crate and kneeled down. The golden retriever huddled in the back corner, but his tail gave the smallest wag when she spoke. "Hey there, sweet boy. You've had a rough time, haven't you?"

Riley crept forward just enough to sniff her fingers through the cage door.

"I have to have him," Emma said suddenly, turning to Kara. "What do I need to do?"

"Well, there's paperwork, and we'll need to do a home visit to make sure everything's in order."

Emma was already nodding. "Where do I fill out the forms?"

"I'll grab them," Kara said.

While Emma waited for the adoption paperwork, Liam made his rounds, saying goodbye to the volunteers and giving each animal a gentle pat.

Charlotte hugged him around the waist. "Will you come back and tell us more stories?"

"Wouldn't miss it."

Later, beside his truck at Emma's house—his old house—the early afternoon sun spilled over the porch where Liam had once sat watching Amelia chase Chip around the yard. She'd run barefoot through the grass, laughing as the dog darted just out of reach. Eventually, she'd catch him, dropping to her knees to wrap her arms around his neck, both of them breathless and grinning. Those were the kinds of afternoons he'd hold on to forever—ordinary moments that meant the world to him.

"I had no idea about all that," Emma said. "About you and Grandma, Tommy, or any of it."

Liam chuckled. "When you get to my age, there's too much to cover in one sitting. Might take another eighty-two years to tell the rest."

Emma laughed, but then her expression grew serious as her eyes moved to the empty spot where Chad's Camaro should have been. "You don't need me to walk you to your truck, do you?"

"I've been walking to this truck longer than you've been alive, Em."

But they both stood there anyway, while Emma's eyes stayed on the forms.

"Chad still at work?"

"Something like that." Emma's shoulders sagged. "We're having some problems, Grandpa. I don't really want to get into it, but ..."

"Your grandma used to say marriage was like a garden.

Some seasons, everything grows easy; other seasons, you work twice as hard just to keep the weeds from taking over."

Emma's gaze met his.

"Thing is, you can't tend a garden by yourself. Takes both people pulling the same way. And if one person stops trying ..."

"I know. I'm just not sure what to do about it."

"You'll figure it out, Em. You're stronger than you think." Liam reached out and squeezed her shoulder. "But no matter what happens, I'll always be here for you."

Emma's eyes filled with tears. "I love you, Grandpa."

"I love you too, kiddo."

She hugged him tight, and for a moment, he was back in another goodbye, another hug, another promise to love no matter what.

Liam climbed into his truck and waved as he pulled away, watching Emma in his rearview mirror until she disappeared around the bend.

He thought about all the people who'd helped him along the way. Ma and Pa, who'd given him everything they could. Simeon, who'd been there when Ma died and had taught him that good work came from the heart as much as the hands. Jerome, always ready with a joke and a helping hand. Mrs. Patterson, who'd fed him and loved him like her own son. Even old Mr. Miller, who'd given him cheaper rent when he'd needed it. And Chip—the constant companion who'd never asked for anything but a scratch behind the ears and whatever scraps were left over.

All of them were gone now, but their kindness had

shaped him into the man he'd become.

And through it all, Amelia. They'd had fifty years together after the wedding. Decades of laughter and tears, arguments and make-ups, quiet mornings and long talks into the night.

Losing her to cancer had been the hardest thing he'd ever faced, and these last years without her had stretched longer than all the rest combined. But he'd had those fifty years with her, and for a boy from Muscadine Drive, that was its own kind of fairy tale.

Liam turned into his driveway as the sun shimmered across the water. Next weekend, he'd go back to the rescue, maybe tell another story. There were always more animals who needed love, and always more people who needed to hear that broken things could be mended.

But today, he'd sit on the porch with a glass of sweet tea and remember the summer that had changed everything—and how, sometimes, if you were lucky, the life you lived turned out even better than the one you'd dreamed.

I hope you enjoyed the story, and though this is the final book in the Hadley Cove Sweet Romance series, the feel-good stories are far from over! Come join us in Sugarberry Ridge!

Binge the Sugarberry Ridge Holiday Romance series for up to 40% off!

Bundle & Save at kerkmurray.com.

**Apply this coupon at checkout
for an additional 10% off: HOLIDAY10**

**Welcome home to Sugarberry Ridge, where
the greatest gifts aren't found under the
tree—they're found in each other.**

Love this book? Don't forget to leave a review!

Help others discover the *Hadley Cove Sweet Romance* series. Every review matters and it matters a lot. It can be as short as one phrase to a few sentences. Wherever you bought this book, you can use this link to leave an honest review on Amazon, Goodreads, Bookbub, or your favorite retailer:

kerkmurray.com/products/reviewsincethedaywepromised

Hadley Cove Recipes

All recipes are vegan-friendly

<u>Ma's Maple Pecan Muffins</u>

The muffins Ma made after Liam and Amelia brought her pecans from their tree.

Ingredients:

- 2 cups all-purpose flour

- 2 teaspoons baking powder

- 1/2 teaspoon salt

- 1/2 cup vegan butter or coconut oil, melted

- 3/4 cup plant-based milk (oat or soy work well)

- 1/3 cup pure maple syrup

- 1 tablespoon ground flaxseed mixed with 3 tablespoons water (let sit 5 minutes)

- 1 teaspoon vanilla extract

- 3/4 cup chopped pecans

- 2 tablespoons maple syrup (for drizzling)

Directions:

1. Preheat oven to 375°F. Grease a 12-cup muffin tin or line with paper cups.

2. In a large bowl, whisk together flour, baking powder, and salt.

3. In a separate bowl, combine melted vegan butter, plant-based milk, 1/3 cup maple syrup, flax mixture, and vanilla. Whisk until well blended.

4. Pour the wet ingredients into the dry ingredients and gently fold together until just combined. Don't overmix.

5. Fold in 1/2 cup of the chopped pecans, reserving the rest for topping.

6. Divide batter evenly among muffin cups, filling each about 2/3 full.

7. Sprinkle remaining pecans on top of each muffin.

8. Bake for 18-22 minutes, or until tops are golden brown and a toothpick inserted in center comes out clean.

9. Cool in pan for 5 minutes, then turn out onto a wire rack.

10. While still warm, drizzle with remaining 2 tablespoons maple syrup.

Ma's Oatmeal Pecan Cookies

Simple, hearty cookies made with love and whatever Ma had on hand.

Ingredients:

- 1 cup all-purpose flour

- 1 teaspoon baking soda

- 1/2 teaspoon salt

- 1/2 teaspoon ground cinnamon

- 1/2 cup vegan butter, softened

- 1/2 cup packed brown sugar

- 1/4 cup granulated sugar

- 1 tablespoon ground flaxseed mixed with 3 tablespoons water (let sit 5 minutes)

- 1 teaspoon vanilla extract

- 1 1/2 cups old-fashioned rolled oats

- 3/4 cup chopped pecans

- 2 tablespoons plant-based milk (if needed)

Directions:

1. Preheat oven to 350°F. Line baking sheets with parchment paper or lightly grease.

2. In a medium bowl, whisk together flour, baking soda, salt, and cinnamon. Set aside.

3. In a large bowl, cream together softened vegan butter, brown sugar, and granulated sugar until light and fluffy, about 3 minutes.

4. Beat in flax mixture and vanilla extract until well combined.

5. Gradually mix in the flour mixture until just combined.

6. Stir in oats and chopped pecans. If dough seems too dry, add plant-based milk one tablespoon at a time.

7. Drop rounded tablespoons of dough onto prepared baking sheets, spacing about 2 inches apart.

8. Bake for 12-15 minutes, or until edges are lightly golden brown but centers still look slightly soft.

9. Let cool on baking sheet for 5 minutes before transferring to a wire rack.

10. Store in an airtight container for up to one week.

Ma's Blue Ribbon Peach Pie

The prize-winning pie that made Ma so proud at the Hadley Cove Fair.

Ingredients:

Crust:

- 2 1/2 cups all-purpose flour

- 1 teaspoon salt

- 1 tablespoon granulated sugar

- 1 cup vegan butter or shortening, cold and cubed

- 6-8 tablespoons ice water

Filling:

- 6-7 large ripe peaches, peeled and sliced

- 3/4 cup granulated sugar

- 1/4 cup packed brown sugar

- 3 tablespoons all-purpose flour

- 1/2 teaspoon ground cinnamon

- 1/4 teaspoon ground ginger

- 1/4 teaspoon salt

- 2 tablespoons vegan butter, cut into small pieces

- 2 tablespoons plant-based milk (for brushing)

Directions:

1. Make the crust: In a large bowl, whisk together flour, salt, and sugar. Cut in cold vegan butter until mixture resembles coarse crumbs.

2. Gradually add ice water, one tablespoon at a time, mixing gently until dough comes together. Divide in half, wrap in plastic, and chill for 1 hour.

3. Preheat oven to 425°F.

4. Roll out bottom crust and place in a 9-inch pie pan. Roll out top crust and set aside.

5. In a large bowl, combine sliced peaches, both sugars, flour, cinnamon, ginger, and salt. Toss gently until peaches are evenly coated.

6. Fill the pie shell with peach mixture and dot with pieces of vegan butter.

7. Cover with top crust, seal edges, and cut several vents. Brush with plant-based milk.

8. Bake for 15 minutes, then reduce heat to 350°F and bake 35-45 minutes more, until crust is golden and filling is bubbly.

9. Cool on a wire rack for at least 2 hours before serving.

Mrs. Patterson's Buttermilk Biscuits

Flaky, tender biscuits that could heal any hurt.

Ingredients:

- 2 cups all-purpose flour

- 1 tablespoon baking powder

- 1 teaspoon salt

- 1 tablespoon sugar

- 6 tablespoons vegan butter, cold and cubed

- 3/4 cup plant-based buttermilk (3/4 cup plant milk + 1 tablespoon lemon juice, let sit 5 minutes)

- 2 tablespoons melted vegan butter for brushing

Directions:

1. Preheat oven to 425°F.

2. In a large bowl, whisk together flour, baking powder, salt, and sugar.

3. Cut in cold vegan butter until mixture resembles coarse crumbs with some pea-sized pieces.

4. Make a well in center and pour in plant-based but-

termilk. Gently stir until dough just comes together.

5. Turn onto floured surface and gently pat into
3/4-inch thick rectangle.

6. Cut straight down with a floured biscuit cutter or
glass. Don't twist.

7. Place on ungreased baking sheet with sides touching.

8. Brush tops with melted vegan butter.

9. Bake 15-17 minutes until golden brown on top.

10. Brush again with melted butter while warm.

Book Club Questions

If you'd like Kerk to attend your in-person or virtual book club, please contact info@kerkmurray.com.

1. How does Liam's character evolve from the eight-year-old boy we meet in 1948 to the man telling his story in the present day?

2. What role does class difference play in shaping Liam and Amelia's relationship throughout the story?

3. Analyze the dynamics between Liam and his mother. How does her influence shape his values and decisions?

4. Compare Tommy's behavior as a child versus as an adult. What factors contributed to his unchanged character?

5. How does the relationship between Liam and Simeon develop, and what does it represent in

terms of chosen family?

6. Discuss the significance of the pecan tree throughout the story. What does it symbolize at different points?

7. How does the theme of "home" evolve throughout the narrative? What makes a place truly home for Liam?

8. Analyze the role of animals, particularly Chip, in the story. What do they represent beyond companionship?

9. How does the author use weather events, particularly Hurricane Ruth, as both plot devices and metaphors?

10. What does the carved heart with "A + L" represent, and how does its meaning change over time?

11. How does the story address poverty and economic hardship in 1940s rural Georgia?

12. Discuss the impact of World War II on the characters, particularly regarding Liam's father's story.

13. How does the author portray class mobility and the American Dream through Liam's journey?

14. What role does community play in supporting individuals during difficult times?

15. How do societal expectations about marriage and social status affect Amelia's choices?

16. How effective is the frame narrative structure of having elderly Liam tell his story at the animal rescue?

17. Discuss the pacing of the romance. Was the twelve-year separation necessary for the story?

18. How does the author build tension leading up to the yacht scene confrontation?

19. What role does coincidence play in the plot, and do you find it believable?

20. How does the ending balance closure with realism?

21. Was Liam right to expose Tommy's affair publicly on the yacht? Could he have handled it differently?

22. Discuss Liam's decision to save Tommy from drowning despite their history. What does this reveal about his character?

23. How do you evaluate Amelia's choices throughout the story? Was she too passive in her own life?

24. What responsibility do the Jensen parents bear for the way events unfolded?

25. How does the story handle the theme of forgive-

ness, both giving and receiving it?

26. How does the author use sensory details to bring the 1940s-50s setting to life?

27. Discuss the author's use of dialogue. How do speech patterns help establish character and time period?

28. How effective are the transitions between different time periods in the story?

29. What role does foreshadowing play in building reader engagement?

30. What lessons about love, loss, and resilience does this story offer? Which resonated most strongly with you, and why?

GIVING BACK

"Never underestimate the power of a small group of committed people to change the world. In fact, it is the only thing that ever has."

—Margaret Mead

"Together redeeming the lives of animals and ending their suffering through our compassion."

THE LEXI'S LEGACY
FOUNDATION INC

Kerk Murray's readers make a difference. Since the release of his memoir, *Pawprints On Our Hearts*, his generous readers have raised over $20,000 toward the care of abused animals through book proceeds as well as donations to the nonprofit he founded, *The Lexi's Legacy Foundation*. If you feel compelled to donate, you can do so right here:
donorbox.org/everydollarmatters

Here's a list of the animal rescue organizations that readers are supporting monthly through each Kerk Murray book sale:

1. 2nd Street Hooligans Rescue – California

2. Cuddly – California

3. Little Hill Sanctuary – California

4. Love Always Sanctuary – California

5. Sale Ranch Animal Sanctuary – California

6. The Shore Sanctuary – California

7. Viva Global Rescue – California

8. Road To Refuge Animal Sanctuary – Connecticut

9. The Riley Farm Sanctuary – Connecticut

10. Love Life Animal Rescue & Sanctuary – Florida

11. Live Freely Sanctuary – Florida

12. Operation Liberation – Florida

13. SAGE Sanctuary and Gardens for Education – Florida

14. Farm of the Free – Georgia

15. Humane Society Greater Savannah – Georgia

16. Society of Humane Friends of Georgia – Georgia

17. Ruby Slipper Goat Rescue – Kansas

18. Shy 38 Inc. – Kansas

19. Sowa Goat Sanctuary – Massachusetts

20. Angela's Ark – North Carolina

21. Billie's Buddies Animal Rescue – North Carolina

22. Fairytale Farm Animal Sanctuary – North Carolina

23. Blackbird Animal Refuge – New Jersey

24. Broncs and Buns Rescue and Rehab – New Jersey

25. Fawn's Fortress – New Jersey

26. Happily Ever After Farm – New Jersey

27. Goats of Anarchy – New Jersey

28. Maddie & Sven's Rescue Sanctuary – New Jersey

29. Marley Meadows Animal Sanctuary – New Jersey

30. Old Fogey Farm – New Jersey

31. Rancho Relaxo – New Jersey

32. Runaway Farm – New Jersey

33. Troll House Animal Sanctuary – New Jersey

34. Wild Lands Wild Horse Fund – New Jersey

35. Happy Compromise Farm – New York

36. Sleepy Pig Farm Animal Sanctuary – New York

37. Woodstock Farm Sanctuary – New York

38. Enchanted Farm Sanctuary – Oregon

39. Harmony Farm Sanctuary – Oregon

40. Morningside Farm Sanctuary – Oregon

41. Charlie's Army Animal Rescue – Pennsylvania

42. Happy Heart Happy Home Farm & Rescue – Pennsylvania

43. The Philly Kitty Club – Pennsylvania

44. The Misfit Farm – Texas

45. Best Friends Animal Society – Utah

46. Harmony Farm Sanctuary and Wellness Center – Vermont

47. Off The Plate Farm Animal Sanctuary – Vermont

48. Gentle Acres Animal Haven – Virginia

49. Little Buckets Farm Sanctuary – Virginia

About the Author

Kerk Murray is an Amazon Top 50 and Barnes and Noble bestselling author of multiple series: *Dog Lovers, Hadley Cove Sweet Romance, and Sugarberry Ridge Holiday Romance.*

If you're a fan of feel-good, clean and wholesome stories that will leave you uplifted and inspired, then his books are a must-read.

Kerk is romantic at heart, with a passion for celebrating life, love, and the beautiful connections between humans and animals. He's also the founder of *The Lexi's Legacy Foundation*, a 501(c)(3) nonprofit organization committed to ending animal suffering. A portion of his books' proceeds are donated to the nonprofit and together with the support of his readers, the lives of hundreds of abused animals have been changed forever.

Join him on his mission in creating a more compassionate world for all living beings, one heartwarming story at a time.

Follow Kerk on social media and sign up for his mailing list at **kerkmurray.com** to stay updated on his latest releases and sneak peeks into his upcoming works.

amazon.com/stores/Kerk-Murray/author/B09C39NLYT

goodreads.com/author/show/21719388.Kerk_Murray

bookbub.com/profile/kerk-murray

instagram.com/kerkmurray

facebook.com/kerkwrites

tiktok.com/@kerkmurray